A Horseman's Gift

A Horseman's Gift

HORSEMEN OF CROSS ROADS FARM ~ BOOK 2

MYRA JOHNSON

Dedication

Remembering the lovely ladies from the Church at Charlotte Moving On After Moving In class, whose encouragement, support, and prayers blessed me so much as I worked to get this book written. Special thanks to the dedicated ladies of the Prayer Shawl Ministry for the beautiful shawl, which comforted and warmed me as I wrote, and which I keep close at hand every day while in my writing chair. Writing may be a solitary profession, but it definitely is a team effort!

Chapter One

Crazy.

For Nathan Cross, no other word came close to describing the past year. Now all he wanted was to survive this wedding—a *double* wedding, no less!—then figure out what exactly God had in mind for the next stage of his life.

Which wasn't exactly turning out the way he'd planned.

Needing some space, he carried his plate of hickory-smoked Texas-style barbecue to the far edge of the covered arena. Today the building was decked out like an open-air reception hall, complete with tarps covering the ground, ribbons and bows festooning the rafters, and a couple dozen banquet tables laid with white tablecloths, candles, and towering floral centerpieces. Apparently, God had smiled upon the happy couples, because the weather had turned out mild and sunny, a perfect August day in the Carolinas.

"Nathan, there you are." A firm female hand clamped down on his arm, nearly causing him to drop his plate. "It's almost time for the best man's toast."

"Already?" Nathan spun around to face Cheri

McNamara, the bespectacled wedding planner, and stifled a sudden attack of the jitters. Okay, he hadn't been all that surprised when the family's barn manager, Kip Lorimer, had asked him to stand up with him when he married Nathan's sister, Sheridan.

But his real wake-up call had come when his own mother asked him to walk her down the aisle to wed Kip's friend, horse breeder Tom Jacobs, soon to whisk Mom away to an East Texas ranch somewhere outside Nacogdoches.

Thanks a lot, Kip.

"You *do* have your speech written out?" The wedding planner's crisp words snapped Nathan out of his pity party.

And after he'd promised himself he'd be happy for Mom and Sheridan no matter how much it seemed as if they'd moved on without him.

He patted the breast pocket of his tux. "Right here, Cheri. No sweat."

"Then I suggest you ditch the barbecue, rinse the coleslaw out of your teeth, and join the happy couples at the head table." Leaning over Nathan's plate, Cheri wrinkled her nose. "What is it with these Texans and their beef? Don't they know we Southerners prefer pulled pork?"

Actually, Nathan was developing an affinity for the taste of slow-grilled beef brisket.

Thanks again, Kip. This time he meant it.

Truth was he had quite a bit to thank Kip for, and he only hoped he could make it through his speech without stumbling over his words or—heaven forbid—getting a little misty-eyed.

He handed Cheri his plate of food and went to rejoin the wedding party.

As he wove his way between the guests' tables, a woman rose from her chair directly in his path. Lustrous black hair cascaded down her back. A deep violet dress draped her curves in something soft and sleek.

Nathan resisted the urge to run a finger around the inside of his suddenly too tight collar. "Uh, excuse me."

The woman whipped around with a gasp. "Oh, sorry—" Her lips spread into a delighted smile. "Nathan!"

"Fil?" When did his voice revert to a prepubescent squeak? "Wow. You look . . . fabulous."

"You too." She lowered thick lashes briefly, then grinned up at him. "Guess we've both come a long way from throwing corn cobs at each other from the hayloft."

Filipa Beltran, the stable hand's daughter and Nathan's best friend growing up. Where had the years gone? "I didn't see you at the wedding. When did you get here?"

"Just a few minutes ago." She gave a one-shoulder shrug. "Car trouble on the drive down. I didn't get in until early this afternoon."

A strangely pleasant tingle started deep within Nathan's chest. Wow, this was *not* the skinny girl in dusty jeans he remembered. After high school he'd hardly seen Filipa. He'd headed off to North Carolina State University in Raleigh. The following year, she'd been accepted by some fancy music school in New York. "How long are you in town? Just for the wedding?"

Filipa's lips flattened. She glanced away before turning a smile on Nathan that hinted at far more than her lilting reply: "No, I'll be home indefinitely."

"Then maybe—"

"Nathan!" Cheri McNamara inserted herself between them and jammed a stiff index finger at her watch face. "We have a schedule to keep."

Nathan shot Filipa an apologetic frown. "Best man duties await. Catch you later?"

She sighed. "I'll be around."

Why didn't he like the sound of that? Okay, he liked the *idea* of her being around just fine. It was the tone in her voice he didn't like. World-weary. Dispirited. Maybe even a bit cynical.

But with Cheri nudging him ever closer to the head table, he didn't have time for further analysis. Now he had to pull out all the stops on his charm and wit and send his mom and sister into their newly married lives in typical Nathan Cross style.

Filipa strode toward the Crosses' back door, careful her stiletto heels didn't sink into the lawn and send her sprawling. Inside the house, she reached the powder room only to find it occupied. As familiar with the Crosses' home as she was her own, she detoured to the bathroom upstairs.

After freshening her lipstick and running a brush through her hair, she couldn't resist a peek into Nathan's room—except obviously it hadn't been Nathan's in quite some time. Instead of baseball pennants, model cars, and piles of dirty clothes, the room looked decidedly feminine . . . if still a bit untidy. And clearly the new occupant was a horse lover. Classic posters from movies like *Secretariat*, *National Velvet*, and *The Black Stallion* adorned walls now painted a restful shade of lavender.

"You lost or something?"

Filipa spun around. The youthful voice belonged to a teenage girl with strawberry-blond hair and a suspicious stare. "I was just admiring your posters," Filipa explained. "I'm an old friend of Nathan's. This used to be his room."

The girl's pursed-lipped frown softened into a smile of

recognition. "You must be Manuelo's daughter. I'm Grace Lorimer. Kip's my big brother."

"Yes, my parents wrote me about you." Father deceased, mother in and out of rehab like a revolving door. "Living here with your brother and the Crosses, you couldn't be in a better place."

"No kidding. I love the horses, plus I get to help with the kids and therapy classes."

Filipa trailed her fingers along the side of a shiny gold equestrian trophy and suffered a frisson of envy. All those years when she could have been riding or volunteering here at the Crosses' equine therapy center . . . stuck in a closet-sized practice room with a metronome and a fusty old music instructor.

Grace peered into the dresser mirror and tucked a loose strand of hair into her French braid. "Guess you heard Nathan will be moving into the caretaker's cottage as soon as Kip and Sheridan leave on their honeymoon."

"Really?"

"Yeah, it's kind of like fruit-basket upset around here. Mrs. Cross—I guess it's Mrs. *Jacobs* now—moving to Texas. Nathan moving out of the house. Kip and Sheridan moving in." Grace huffed a light laugh. "At least I get to keep my room."

The distant drone from the country-western band rose to a crescendo and then faded into silence. Filipa gave a start. "That sounds like a signal for something important. We should probably get back to the reception."

By the time Filipa rejoined her family at their table, Nathan was glibly introducing the various members of the wedding party. She couldn't get over how James-Bond tall, dark, and handsome he looked in his tux. She leaned toward her father. "Nathan looks really good."

Understatement of the century. "How's he handling his mother's remarriage?"

Manuelo Beltran gave his daughter a weak smile. "Not so good, I think. He still misses his father."

"I'm sure." Mr. Cross had passed away not quite three years ago, a shock to everyone who knew him. Filipa could only imagine how hard it must be for Nathan to see his mother moving on with someone new—not to mention marrying off both his mother and sister on the same day! At least both couples appeared deliriously happy and very, *very* much in love.

Again, an inescapable sense of loss engulfed Filipa. She had made music her life . . . and now she didn't even *have* a life.

Well, that was about to change. She hadn't yet found the time or the courage to inform her parents, but she'd made up her mind she would not return to New York. In fact, right now she didn't care if she never picked up her guitar again.

"Not return to New York?" Filipa's father hammered the kitchen countertop with his fist. "Of *course* you will continue your music studies. This is what you have worked so hard for all your life!"

"Calm down, Manuelo." Filipa's mother carried a platter of baked chicken to the table. "Filipa is a grown woman. She has a right to make her own decisions." Mama narrowed one eye as she returned to the stove for the vegetables. "Even if those decisions are perhaps not the wisest."

Filipa offered a grudging smile. "Thank you, Mama."

"Do not take her side in this, Rosa." Her father thudded into his chair and crossed his arms. "No daughter of mine will spit in the face of her God-given talents!"

Filipa's teenage brother Carlos—or Charlie, as he preferred to be called—slid into his chair with a scowl. "If Fil's not going back to New York, does that mean I have to give back her room? Because I'm *not* moving back in with Joseph. He snores!"

"The sofa's fine for now." Filipa rolled her eyes at her father. "Anyway, it's my *just deserts* for breaking my parents' hearts."

Her father launched into a spate of Spanish that Filipa couldn't keep up with even though she'd been raised bilingual. But words like *decepción* and *muerte* were hard to miss. Apparently she was a huge *disappointment* and would surely be the *death* of her humble, hardworking parents.

"Enough, Manuelo." Mama set a basket of rolls in the center of the table. "Filipa, sit down and eat. We'll have no more of this bickering on the Lord's Day. Charlie, you may offer thanks since your father is too angry to address the Lord with humility."

While Charlie said grace, Filipa glanced around the table at her family—Papa, Mama, Charlie, Naomi, Elisa, and Joseph, the youngest. They were a proud family, demonstrative in their affections, devoted to each other and to the Lord. Filipa loved them with all her heart.

But not enough to return to the rigors of music school, no matter how vehemently her father insisted. She'd sooner spend the rest of her life helping Mama with her housecleaning business or working alongside Papa while he mucked out horse stalls.

Later, with the lemony fragrance of dishwashing

bubbles tickling her nose, Filipa heard the phone ring. Charlie yelled through the kitchen door. "It's for you, Fil."

Who even knew she was in town? Must be someone she'd run into at the wedding reception yesterday. She dried her hands before snatching up the kitchen extension. "Hello?"

"Hey, Fil. What's up?"

Her heart gave an unnerving little skitter. "Nathan? I thought you'd have left for Raleigh by now. Don't you have an internship to get back to?"

"I've got another few hours. You have plans? We hardly had a chance to catch up yesterday."

Filipa draped the dishtowel over the oven door handle. "I could come over to your place. It's getting a little crowded around here."

"Great. See you in a few."

Minutes later, Filipa had traded her slip-on sneakers for an ancient pair of scuffed boots. Maybe with a little sweet-talking she could convince Nathan to saddle up a couple of horses. Being back at Cross Roads Farm and then seeing those posters in Grace's room yesterday had awakened a childhood longing Filipa had been forced to suppress but had never outgrown.

"You are destined for better things, mija. *You have the gift of music. No daughter of mine will spend her life as a laborer."*

Dear Papa, so proud. Stubbornly proud. Filipa knew he only wanted his children to have a better life than he had known—the poverty of growing up in Mexico, the struggle to gain U.S. citizenship, then backbreaking labor at minimum wage to eke out a living for his family.

At least until he made his way to Cross Roads Farm and Nathan's father hired him as a stable hand. The Crosses had been good to the Beltrans, made sure they found a place to live only a mile or so from the farm, treated the Beltran kids like their own.

But that didn't change the fact that Filipa's skin would always be a few shades darker than Nathan's, or make it any easier for non-Hispanics to pronounce her name correctly (what was so hard about *Fi-LEE-pa*?). She appreciated her parents' efforts to instill a strong work ethic in their children, to encourage them to rise above their circumstances, but sometimes they pushed too hard.

And Filipa had had enough. For a while, at least, she intended to kick back and do absolutely nothing that wasn't her choice and hers alone.

Chapter Two

One hip propped against the counter in the spacious country kitchen, Nathan munched on crackers and pimiento cheese and hoped Fil arrived soon. It was way too quiet around here. With the newlyweds off on their honeymoons and Grace staying in town with church friends until Kip and Sheridan returned, the old farmhouse echoed with the emptiness.

He should be spending today packing up his things in the downstairs guest room he'd taken over last year after his riding accident and then Grace's entry into their lives. Kip and Sheridan sure didn't need him underfoot once they moved in. Ever since completing his business degree at NC State last May and then accepting an internship at a prestigious technology firm in Raleigh, Nathan had been praying for a paying position to open up within the company. An entry-level management job with BBJ Systems, Inc., would have gone a long way toward launching him into his dream career as a big-time business mogul.

What he *hadn't* expected was that his widowed mother

would fall in love with a cowboy, marry the guy barely one year later, and then inform Nathan she intended to turn over the administration of their equine therapy center to him.

Mom could be downright bossy at times, but her faith in Nathan massaged his ego in ways he couldn't express. How could he say no, when he now had both the education and a summer of on-the-job training to prepare him for such a responsibility? Not to mention the fact that Cross Roads Farm was his late father's dream. If for no other reason, he'd do this for his dad.

Knuckles tapped on the glass in the back door. Brushing cracker crumbs off his chin, Nathan pulled open the door, his gaze sweeping Filipa's curvy, blue-jeaned figure. Once again, he was reminded that the little girl he used to ride bikes and do homework with was all grown up!

He swallowed and tried for a nonchalant grin, hoping to conceal his unexpected—and very grown-up—attraction. "Hey, Fil, come on in."

Hands stuffed in her pockets, Filipa scuffed one boot on the doorsill. "Could we go see the horses? Papa mentioned awhile back that Mr. Jacobs had brought you a new one."

"Ember. Yeah, he's terrific. Sure, let's head out to the barn." An idea that was sounding better and better. All things considered, Nathan decided a walk in the great outdoors was the wisest course of action.

Filipa fell into step beside Nathan as they crossed the lawn. "You still have Jet, though? I can't imagine you'd ever part with your dad's pride and joy."

"Not a chance. But Jet belongs to Kip now. My accident forced me to admit Jet is way more horse than I can handle."

"I was so worried when I heard what happened—and so relieved it wasn't anything worse."

"Me, too." Nathan rubbed his neck. He still cringed when he thought about how close he'd come to being paralyzed for life.

They strode through the main barn and then through a smaller barn. In the paddock beyond, two geldings grazed, chomping and tearing at thick, green tufts of grass. Ember, the smaller of the two, whinnied and strode over to the fence. Nathan reached into his pocket for one of the peppermints he always kept handy, unwrapped it, and offered it to the horse. Crunching on the candy, Ember bobbed his head in appreciation.

"Wow, he's adorable." Laughing, Filipa reached out to stroke Ember's muzzle. She nodded toward the big black horse still nibbling on grass. "Ember and Jet must get along okay."

"Ember's definitely a calming influence. Jet's thunderstorm freak-outs have been a lot less severe since Ember moved in." Either that or it was all Kip's doing. Nathan continually stood in awe of the quiet horseman who'd come into their lives just over a year ago. Yep, awe and no small amount of envy. Nathan's attitude had improved a lot since then, but it still rankled that Kip could do things with Jet that Nathan could never dream of.

"Do you think . . ." Filipa angled Nathan a hopeful smile. "I mean, if you have time . . . could we maybe go riding?"

Nathan checked his watch. He could leave by five or six and still make it to Raleigh in time to finish up some last-minute prep work before he reported to the office tomorrow.

And besides, going horseback riding with Filipa Beltran

on a balmy summer afternoon was suddenly the only thing on earth he wanted to do.

Twenty minutes later, Filipa finished brushing down a flyspecked gray named Gem. The sweet-natured horse, smelling of barn dust and hay, nuzzled Filipa's side as she tossed the brush into the grooming tote. She gave Gem's neck a hug, the sheer joy of being around horses again making her almost woozy.

Nathan finished tacking Ember, then carried over a black neoprene sports saddle for Gem. Filipa stepped to the horse's other side to smooth out the fleece pad before Nathan hefted the saddle onto the horse's back.

After tightening the cinch, he handed Filipa the reins and then bustled into the tack room, returning moments later with two riding helmets. "Safety first, you know."

"Cross Roads Farm rule—how could I forget?" She donned the smaller helmet and fastened the clasp beneath her chin. "I assume you still have my old release on file?"

"Since Mom never throws anything important away, I'm sure we do." Nathan grinned. "Except I'm betting it was signed by your dad a million years ago when you were still a minor."

Filipa slapped his arm. "Hey, I'm not *that* old!"

"Yeah, well, remind me to have you sign your own release before I take you riding again." He formed a cradle with his laced fingers. "Give you a leg up?"

Gripping the pommel, Filipa braced her left knee in Nathan's hands and hoped he didn't notice how his closeness made her suck in a breath. With a one-two-three he boosted her into the saddle, then checked and adjusted her stirrup lengths. Tingles raced through her limbs as he tugged the wrinkles out of her pant legs and positioned her feet in the stirrups.

He patted her shin. "Good?"

She swallowed, nodded, and managed a smile. "Good."

"Good." Nathan unclipped Ember from the cross ties and swung into his English jumping saddle with the grace of a man who'd spent his life around horses.

A mixture of envy and admiration squeezed her throat. "You look good up there."

His dimples deepened. "You look pretty good, yourself."

A laugh burst from Filipa's throat. "My *good*ness, are we a mutual admiration society or what?"

Nathan beamed a mile-wide grin as he nudged his horse into a walk. "I've really missed your laugh."

His words, his smile, the sunshine caressing their shoulders, the horse scent wafting into the air . . . Filipa warmed with delicious memories of simpler times—days of freedom, innocence, a whole world of possibilities before them. A clutch in her heart made it hard to breathe. She wanted to say, *And I've missed laughing*, but if she opened her mouth to speak, she feared all the emotions she'd been holding inside for so long would gush out in an unstoppable torrent.

Several steps ahead now, Nathan peered over his shoulder. "You forget how to make a horse go?"

Snapping out of her reverie, Filipa laughed again, relishing the echo in her ears, the jolt to her lungs. "Are you kidding? Bet I can still beat you to the creek!"

She gave Gem a firm squeeze with her calves, and the gray swept past Nathan and Ember in a smooth, rocking-horse canter.

"You rat!" Nathan's voice rang out behind her. "Never did play fair!"

Down the pebbled lane, through open gates where pastures stood empty, between oaks and maples and sweet gums . . . soon Filipa's horse splashed through the stream at the far edge of the Crosses' property. She hunched forward to duck beneath a low-hanging limb as Gem climbed the slope. Breathless, she turned her horse and looked for Nathan.

Nathan reined Ember up short on the other side of the creek. "That's still old Emma Webber's property. You know how she feels about trespassers."

Filipa glanced over her shoulder in a panic, as if the grouchy old woman might be right behind her with a shotgun. How could she forget the time Mrs. Webber had caught her and Nathan playing hide-and-seek in her peach orchard? Never so scared in her life, Filipa had raced all the way home, never even looking back to see if Nathan followed.

And then she was too embarrassed to look him in the eye when she boarded the school bus the next morning.

After a hurried retreat to Nathan's side of the creek, Filipa released her pent-up breath. But as she perused their surroundings, something struck her as odd. "Wait a minute. The Webber property doesn't begin until that tree line." She pointed a good quarter-mile east of where they stood. "Across the creek here is still your land."

"Gotcha!" Nathan grinned. "Wish I'd had my camera to capture the look on your face."

She glared. "Nathan Cross, if you hadn't grown so much since junior high, I'd wipe that snarky smile right off your face."

And I'd gladly let you try.

Nathan could hardly believe the effect an all-grown-up Filipa Beltran was having on him, but he wished with all his being he didn't have to finish packing and then drive back to Raleigh. He'd like to hang around and continue getting to know her all over again.

A regretful sigh hissed between his lips. "Ready to head back?"

"Guess we should."

Did Filipa seem as reluctant to end the day as he? His thoughts zipped back to yesterday at the reception and how melancholy she'd sounded uttering those words, *"I'll be around."*

Their horses fell in step together, but this time Nathan made sure they kept to a leisurely walk. No point in drawing the afternoon to a close any sooner than necessary. He slanted his gaze in Filipa's direction. "You said yesterday you'd be home for a while. What exactly is *a while*? Don't you have to get back to school?"

The flattened lips and subtle stiffening of her spine suggested she'd rather not talk about it. "I'm . . . taking a sabbatical."

A sabbatical. Did musicians do that? Didn't they have to practice constantly to maintain their proficiency? "I thought you loved music."

Definitely forbidden territory, judging by the look in her eyes. If Filipa had access to Mrs. Webber's shotgun right now, he'd most likely be staring down the business end of the barrel.

He changed his tactics. "Look, Fil, I don't mean to pry, but . . . I just don't get it."

"There's nothing to *get*." Filipa pushed the words out like glue from a dried-out tube. "I needed a break. Can we leave it at that?"

"So this is temporary, right? I mean, you haven't given up on your music career?"

Gem stumbled on a fallen limb, and Filipa reached down to pat his neck. "Easy, boy. Watch your step."

Was she talking to the horse, or to Nathan? He decided maybe he should cool the third degree until he knew for sure.

In the meantime, he should probably close some pasture gates behind them. Letting Filipa go on ahead, he circled back and latched the last gate they'd passed through. He caught up with her in time to see her dabbing moist cheeks against the sleeve of her T-shirt.

He reined Ember close enough that he could seize Filipa's hand. "Talk to me, Fil. What's really going on?"

"I'm sick of the pressure, okay?" A brain-rattling sniffle shook her. She tugged her hand free of his and scrubbed a silky strand of dark hair off her face. "Know anyone who's in the market for a slightly used—make that *extremely* used—Paulino Bernabe classical guitar?"

Nathan's jaw dropped. "You're not serious."

Her snapping gaze told him she was dead serious.

Hands tightening on the reins, he yanked Ember to a halt. "You'd throw away your scholarships, your future? What about everything your parents have sacrificed to bring you this far? Can you really walk away from music like all those years of lessons and practice meant nothing?"

"It isn't my responsibility to fulfill my parents' dreams." Filipa urged her horse into a trot, increasing the distance between them.

As if the gulf could get any wider. Nathan's gut

clenched. Here he was, more committed than ever to preserving his father's dream for Cross Roads Farm. Filipa, on the other hand, seemed bent on throwing her parents' hopes, plans, and hard work back in their faces. Maybe he didn't know Filipa as well as he imagined.

Maybe he didn't *want* to.

Chapter Three

"So it's hopeless?" Filipa chewed her lip as she stood outside the bay where a mechanic had spent the last three hours fiddling with her 1994 Honda Civic.

"Starter's shot, alternator's fried, radiator's near rusted out—and that's just gettin' started." The mechanic wiped his hands on a greasy rag. "Yeah, unless you got a couple grand to spend on repairs, I'd say it's hopeless."

Guess she couldn't complain. The car already had nearly 80,000 miles on it when Papa bought it for her in high school. Add two or three trips a year between Kingsley and New York for the past few years, plus regular excursions for master classes, music festivals, auditions, and concerts, and it was a wonder the car had held up this long.

Great. Just what she needed. Back in town for over two weeks now and still no job leads. She'd planned to drive into Charlotte tomorrow and follow up on the substitute teacher applications she'd dropped off last week, then maybe scout around for a cheap one-bedroom apartment. Living under her parents' roof grew more unpleasant every day.

But it all came down to money. Until she landed a regular, decent-paying job, she was stuck.

Stuck with Papa's accusing glares.

Stuck with Mama's pouty frowns.

Stuck camping out on the living-room sofa while Charlie's rock music blared from the speakers of *her* stereo in *her* room.

Guilt pretzeled her stomach. There remained one way she could easily score enough cash to tide her over for at least a couple of months—*sell her guitar*.

She squeezed her eyes shut and imagined the honey-colored, satiny-smooth German spruce body, the curve of the figured rosewood side nesting against her thigh. The tension of strings beneath her fingers, each note resonating with rich clarity—

"Miz Beltran? You make up your mind?"

Her eyes popped open to meet the mechanic's impatient gaze. Massaging the calluses on the tips of her fingers, she let her shoulders droop. "Any chance you'd buy the car for parts?"

The mechanic entered the bay to give the Honda one last perusal. Rejoining Filipa outside, he shrugged and named a figure far less than the value of her cherished Paulino Bernabe.

She heaved a breath. "I'll take it."

Even if she never picked up her guitar again, she couldn't easily part with the object that symbolized half her life. Bad enough Nathan had to remind her of how much her parents had sacrificed on her behalf. But Filipa had also scrimped and saved, working after-school and summer jobs to subsidize music lessons while putting aside every spare dollar toward replacing the scarred, twangy, fourth-hand Gibson guitar she'd learned on.

Her savings wouldn't have been nearly enough for the Bernabe even then, if not for an anonymous benefactor. One day shortly after her high school graduation, a letter had arrived from a prestigious guitar shop near the music school where she'd been accepted:

> Five thousand dollars has been placed on account for you toward the purchase of the instrument of your choice. Please come in at your earliest convenience to make your selection from our fine selection of classical guitars.

Five thousand dollars. From a perfect stranger. Or at least someone who intended to protect his identity. A stranger whose generosity now hammered yet another nail in the lid of her coffin of guilt.

Walking out of the car repair shop with three plastic bags bulging with items she'd rescued from her trunk and glove compartment, plus a meager check that *might* cover half a month's apartment rent, Filipa strode up Kingsley's main drag toward the bank. After depositing the money into her account, she stepped onto the sidewalk and fished her cell phone from her purse. Somehow, somewhere, she needed to finagle a ride home.

"Filipa?"

Glancing up, she looked into the beaming face of Nathan's sister. "Sheridan! Wow, you look fantastic! Are you back from your honeymoon already?"

"Just yesterday." One arm looped through the handles of a huge Kingsley Mercantile shopping bag, Sheridan flicked at pale blond bangs. "I was picking up some late wedding gifts at the Merc and thought I recognized you coming out of the bank."

Filipa smirked and tilted her head toward her armload of plastic bags. "Yep, just sold my junk heap of a car."

"Time for an upgrade, huh? You've been driving that Honda forever!"

"Actually . . . I have no idea what I'm going to do for transportation until I can replenish my savings."

Sheridan's forehead wrinkled. "Is that why you're still in town? I thought you'd be back in New York by now."

Fatigue saddled Filipa's shoulders. She did *not* feel like explaining all over again why she wasn't returning to music school. Then, to make matters worse, her lower lip started trembling and tears squeezed from her eyes.

Sheridan dropped her shopping bag and pulled Filipa into a comforting hug. "Oh, honey, what's wrong?"

Filipa broke free and swiped at her cheeks. Rebalancing her bags of car stuff, she forced a crooked smile. "Want to have lunch? I could sure use a sympathetic ear."

Ten minutes later, a Kingsley Station hostess seated them in a quiet booth overlooking the train tracks behind the building, an old railway station converted to a charmingly decorated restaurant that served the best homestyle cooking this side of Charlotte.

As soon as their server left with their orders, Sheridan lasered Filipa with her crystal-blue gaze. "All right, girlfriend, time to spill."

Filipa sipped her water. "Just don't lecture me, okay? Your little brother already did a good job of that."

"Nathan lectured you? When? Why?"

"The day after your wedding." Filipa pursed her lips. "After I told him I was giving up my music career."

Sheridan gaped for a full three seconds before clamping her jaw shut. She closed her eyes and inhaled slowly through her nostrils while tapping shiny pink nails on the table. When she opened her eyes again, her lips softened into a concerned smile. "We've known each other for ages, Fil. You're smart, determined, as dedicated to your dreams as anyone I've ever known. So I have to believe you didn't make this decision lightly. What I *don't* understand is why."

Filipa bit the inside of her lip to keep from crying again, but she couldn't stop the sigh that started in her toes and came out in a trembling gush. "I'm tired, Sher. I'm just . . . so tired."

The server returned with a grilled chicken salad for Sheridan and a turkey-avocado croissant sandwich for Filipa. They spent a few moments organizing condiments and utensils, and Filipa took advantage of the respite to compose herself. She could tell by the firm set of Sheridan's mouth that her friend wouldn't rest until Filipa explained further.

Sheridan drizzled honey-mustard dressing over her salad and then poked at the greens with her fork. "Honestly, Fil, I can't even imagine the commitment it takes to become a professional musician. I do remember how hard you worked all through high school, how we hardly ever saw you at the farm once you began music lessons in earnest. Nathan moped around for months."

"He did?" Filipa forced down a bite of croissant.

"You two were best friends." Sheridan raised a disbelieving brow. "What did you expect?"

Truth be told, she'd been so wrapped up in school, part-time jobs, and music lessons that she'd barely had time to even think about Nathan.

But that gorgeous afternoon horseback riding with him a couple of weeks ago had been oh-so-nice.

At least until he'd shut her out. Returning to the barn that day, they'd exchanged little more than polite nods as they untacked their horses and turned them out to pasture. Every huffed breath, every slanted look, every muscle twitch had evidenced Nathan's extreme disapproval.

Sheridan sliced through a strip of grilled chicken and then chewed thoughtfully. "So if you're not going back to New York, what *are* your plans?"

"Find a job, get my own place, pick up a cheap used car somewhere." Filipa pushed her barely touched sandwich aside and gazed out the window. "That's about as far ahead as I've allowed myself to think."

"Wish I knew what to suggest, but my brain is still fried from planning a wedding." Sheridan laughed softly. "Who'd have thought my mom and I would *both* be getting married this summer?"

Relieved to change the subject, Filipa rested an elbow on the table. "So tell me more about these handsome cowboys who swept you and your mother off your feet."

Sheridan's eyes gleamed as the words rushed out. She told how Kip Lorimer had driven all the way from Texas last year to donate Gem, the horse Filipa had ridden that day with Nathan. Remorse filled Sheridan's face as she described her lack of trust and how hard Kip had to work to break down her defenses. Then, when his friend Tom Jacobs delivered Ember for Nathan, romance had blossomed between Tom and Sheridan's mother.

"I didn't want to renege on my special-ed teaching commitment for last year," Sheridan explained, "so Kip and I weren't planning to marry until June at the earliest. But then Mom and Tom started getting serious, and the idea of a double wedding came up, so we finally all settled on the August date." Sheridan beamed. "And it was definitely worth waiting for!"

"What a sweet story. I'm so happy for both of you—for

all of you." Filipa blinked several times, tamping down another twinge of envy. She *was* happy for her friends.

And maybe, now that she actually had time and space in her life for romance, it would finally happen for her.

One foot propped on a chair rung, the other leg stretched beneath a cafeteria lunch table, Nathan pounded keys on his laptop to complete a report his boss had requested. A sudden vibration in his breast pocket nearly toppled him out of his seat—his smartphone alarm reminding him lunch break was over. Gathering up his laptop and a stack of file folders with one hand, scrambling to silence his phone with the other, he made a less than graceful exit.

On his way through the lobby, his cell phone vibrated again, this time with a call from Kip. "Hey, bro. How's married life treating you?"

"Fine, just fine." Kip's lazy Texas drawl sounded even mellower than usual. "You should try it sometime."

"I plan to. Once I get moved back from Raleigh and figure out what I'm supposed to be doing as CEO of Cross Roads Farm." He snorted, would have snapped his fingers if he wasn't juggling a phone and his laptop. "Oh, and did I leave out one *really* important factor, as in meeting the right girl?"

"You will. Count on it."

Not a conversation Nathan felt like having at the moment. Memories of his recent Sunday outing with Fil still nagged at him. How could an afternoon that began with so much promise have ended so badly?

He checked his watch. Five minutes before his meeting with the boss. "Prying conversation out of you is like talking to a feed bucket, so I know you didn't call to shoot the breeze. You need advice about Sheridan?" He snickered. "Want to know where I stowed the Scrabble game?"

"Not hardly!" Kip guffawed, a rare sound from the soft-spoken cowboy. Clearly, married life agreed with him. "Just lettin' you know Sher and I are back from Puerto Rico. Your mom and Tom are flying in tomorrow after their Hawaii trip, and this weekend we'll be going over some business matters, planning the next volunteer orientation, and laying out the fall class schedule. I figured you'd want to be here for that."

Except Nathan had way too much work ahead before he wrapped up this internship. He hadn't planned on returning to Kingsley for another couple of weeks. He pushed the elevator call button. "It'll have to be a quick trip."

"We'll take what we can get."

"Okay, then, I'll be there late Friday." The elevator doors swished open, and Nathan stepped aside as a flirty red-haired intern breezed through the opening. She worked in the office next to Nathan's, and he'd been savoring the scent of her perfume all summer.

Kip spoke into his ear. "Want us to keep some dinner warm for you?"

The leggy redhead flicked the tail of a colorful scarf in Nathan's direction. "Don't bother. I'll grab something on the way down."

Or, if he played his cards right, an early dinner for two right here in Raleigh.

He was a magna cum laude business major, after all, soon to be entrusted with the running of an accredited and highly successful equine therapy center. It sure would be nice to have a sweetheart of his own to sit down to dinner with every evening, an affectionate wife to snuggle with every night. The tiny caretaker's cottage next to the barn could serve as a charming love nest until they were ready to start a family—

"Nathan?" The redhead had backtracked, catching him just as he stepped onto the elevator. Fluttering overly mascaraed lashes, she held the door. "You busy? I could really use some help with this software analysis I've been working on."

Regret corkscrewed through his gut. "Sorry, I'm running late for a meeting. Maybe later?"

Her mouth pushed out in a lovely, lip-glossed pout. "I'll be around."

"I'll be around."

The face of a dark-eyed beauty flashed across Nathan's mind. Skin the color of creamy golden caramels. A mass of ebony tresses cascading down her back. Long, thick lashes so full they didn't even need mascara.

Gritting his teeth, he shoved the image from his mind. No way would he let himself fall for a woman who could so casually toss aside everything she'd worked for, planned for. Everything her parents had sacrificed so that she could fulfill her dream. Everything God had gifted her to become.

Punching the button for the twelfth floor, Nathan decided he'd better forget women for now and maintain focus on his own goal, which was and always would be making his father proud. Nathan would never forget the man who'd told him long ago, *"Son, you don't have to be the best horseman or the best baseball player or the best anything. All that matters to me is that you are the best* Nathan *God created you to be."*

Chapter Four

"Nathan, honey!" The instant he walked through the kitchen door, his mother threw her arms around his middle and squeezed until he gasped for air.

Laughing, he wiggled out of her embrace and lifted an eyebrow in Tom's direction. "What kind of vitamins have you been feeding this woman?"

The Texas horse rancher with a John Wayne physique only grinned, then shared a look with Nathan's mother that set fire to both their faces. Only one word described it: *lovesick.*

Kip's little sister, Grace, finished filling the dogs' water bowl and set it on a mat near the back door. She rolled her eyes at Nathan. "See what I've been putting up with all week?"

Nathan shot her a knowing smirk. He wheeled his weekender suitcase out of the way before shaking Tom's hand. "How was Hawaii? Or do I need to ask?"

"'Bout as good as you might expect." Tom hooked an elbow around his blushing wife's neck and drew her close.

Footsteps sounded on the staircase, and seconds later

Kip and Sheridan strode into the kitchen. Arms locked around each other, they appeared joined at the hip. Man, oh man, what had Nathan gotten himself into, coming home to not one but two newlywed couples still glowing from their honeymoons?

"Thought we heard voices," Kip said. "Welcome home, bro."

Although he did like the sound of that. Nathan couldn't have handpicked a better brother than Kip Lorimer.

Sheridan planted a kiss on Kip's cheek before easing from beneath his arm. She went to the oven and peeked inside, releasing a cheesy-spicy-tomatoey aroma that ignited Nathan's taste buds. "We weren't expecting you until later. Have you had supper?"

He swallowed to keep from drooling. "Uh, nope, just hopped in my car after work and drove straight here." Unfortunately, his dinner plans hadn't panned out. The redhead expected to be slaving away on her software analysis late into the night.

Mom nudged him toward the hallway. "Go get settled and wash up while Sher and I put supper on the table. Afterward, we can get down to business. We've got a lot to accomplish this weekend."

She wasn't kidding. No sooner had they cleared the table after supper than Mom assigned Tom and Grace dishwasher duty, while she, Kip, Sheridan, and Nathan gathered around a worktable in the study. Over the next four hours Nathan got a crash course in equine therapy center management. Already beat from working through lunch so he could leave early and then the three-hour drive from Raleigh, he was ready to call it a night long before his mother declared the proceedings at an end.

By nine o'clock Saturday morning they were hard at it again, just Nathan and his mother this time, and Nathan soon realized how much he'd taken for granted about how hard Mom worked to keep Cross Roads Farm running smoothly and in the black.

Mom angled the computer screen toward Nathan and clicked an icon that brought up a financial program. "With Kip managing the horses and Sheridan handling classes and volunteers, your main focus has to be the money end. Your dad left us pretty well off, so up to now we've been able to cover expenses with the interest from his trust fund, plus tuition payments, donations, and grants. But the tighter the economy gets, the harder it's going to be. You may need to come up with some creative ideas to generate more income."

Nathan rubbed his chin. "Like a fundraiser?"

"Possibly. I've been checking out what other centers are doing—ride-a-thons, auctions, corporate sponsorships, fundraising dinners. Our center is small compared to most, so you'll have to decide what could work best."

The weight of these new responsibilities pressed Nathan into his chair. If he let Mom down . . . if he let *Dad* down . . . could he ever forgive himself?

By noon Nathan was convinced his eyes would fall out of their sockets if he looked at one more procedural guide or computer report. Clawing at his temples, he leaned back in his chair. "Can we take a break, Mom?"

She pursed her lips, those gray-blue eyes laced with apology. "Sorry, son. I know it's a lot to take in."

"I should have been paying more attention all along. I just never expected . . ."

Mom's hand snaked out to capture his. "Never

expected your dad to die so young. Never expected your mother to remarry and move to Texas."

"I'm happy for you, Mom. I really am. But . . ." Nathan turned his mother's hand over, his gaze snagging on the flamboyant diamond ring Tom had given her. He missed seeing the delicate solitaire and simple gold band that for most of Nathan's life had told the world she was Mrs. Kenneth Cross.

His mother sat back, extending her fingers for a split second before tucking both hands beneath her arms. "I've pushed this on you, haven't I? Without so much as a thought for *your* wants and needs."

"Cross Roads Farm is as important to me as it is to you. As it was to Dad. I'm proud and honored you want me to step in." He offered his mother a sad smile. "I just wish you weren't moving a thousand miles away."

Filipa wished she were a thousand miles away.

Or deaf.

Anything, so she wouldn't have to listen to one more of Papa's lectures.

"La, la, la, la." She laid aside the dog-eared paperback mystery she'd been reading and clapped her hands over her ears. "I can't hear you, Papa."

"And now you are being childish." Looming over the sofa where she sat, Papa shook his hands heavenward. "*¡Mija!* When will you come to your senses?"

She strove for composure. "You're right, Papa, I *am* being childish, and I'm sorry." Rising with effort, she stood and faced her father with an imploring gaze. "I don't mean to disrespect you. I only wish you would try to understand."

"What is to understand? You have left your studies—your music—and come home to *this*." He swept his arm in a gesture that took in every inch of their tiny frame house.

Yet Filipa knew he didn't mean just the house, but the life of continual struggle to make ends meet. The life he and Mama had always hoped their children would rise above.

She cupped his weathered cheek, her eyes softening. "Papa, I love you, and I will never be able to repay you for the sacrifices you've made for me, for all us kids. But I need you to stop pushing so hard. I need you to trust me to live my own life."

"Even when I see you are throwing your life away?"

Filipa bit back a crisp retort. "Yes, even then."

Papa dipped his head. "Then it appears there is nothing left for me to do but pray for you."

Which would be so much more helpful than his reproach.

She watched tiredly as her father donned his dusty ball cap and headed out the door for evening chores at Cross Roads Farm, and had no doubt he was already bombarding heaven with his prayers. Filipa, on the other hand, had done far too little praying of late. She'd let the pressures of music school, her parents' expectations, and nagging self-doubt crowd out any sense of the Holy.

On a lamp table near the window, Mama displayed a stylized clay figure of Jesus that had been in her family for three generations, the intricately hand-painted piece having survived the long move north from Mexico. Filipa crossed to the table and caressed the figurine. "Jesus . . . if You're listening . . ." Her voice broke. She brought the little statue to her lips.

A Bible verse from Romans Mama had often recited popped into her mind: *We do not know what we ought to pray for, but the Spirit himself intercedes for us through wordless groans.*

Filipa truly had no idea how she should be praying. Should she ask God to restore her love of music? Or was this increasing sense of discontent God's way of moving her toward a new path?

Maybe some fresh air would bring clarity. She retied the sneakers she'd kicked off earlier and then started down the driveway. If she turned east at the road, her steps would take her past Cross Roads Farm. Not a good idea, since that's where Papa worked. Besides, she'd heard Nathan had come home for the weekend.

The two men most critical of her recent change of plans? She preferred not to run into either one of them just now.

She turned west, but had hardly traveled twenty steps when a brisk wind came up out of nowhere and stripped the September afternoon of its warmth. Shivering in her thin T-shirt, Filipa decided maybe a walk wasn't such a good idea after all. As she circled back toward the house, she could barely see with tangled strands of hair whipping across her face. She stumbled, cracked a knee against the rough pavement, and yelped in pain.

As she pushed to her feet, a car horn sounded. Brakes whined, and the vehicle pulled off to the side of the road. A door slammed. "Fil! You okay?"

Nathan. Her stomach bottomed out. She corralled her blowing hair in one fist and brushed wetness from her cheeks with the other. Not tears. Not in front of Nathan. It was the wind, that's all. And her throbbing knee. "I just tripped. I'm fine."

And then she wasn't fine at all, because Nathan had his arms around her, steadying her, inspecting every inch of her with a look in his deep brown eyes that made her forget her knee, the wind, even her own name.

Seemingly satisfied she wasn't hurt—her pride notwithstanding—Nathan straightened and stuffed his hands into his jeans pockets. "Looked like you hit the pavement pretty hard."

"I'll live." Filipa's knee suddenly reminded her of its presence. She bent down to rub it. So much for a quiet, leisurely walk to clear her head.

Glancing toward his gold Sonata, Nathan heaved a sigh. "Wanna go somewhere? I think we need to talk."

Filipa suddenly noticed the wind had ceased. Coincidence . . . or God's intervention? She finger-combed the knots from her hair. "All right, but no one else is home right now, so give me a sec to leave a note."

Nathan rocked on his heels while he waited for Filipa to return from the house. He couldn't exactly say this stop was planned. But an hour ago, his thoughts churning with all the facts, figures, and instructions Mom had filled his head with, he'd decided to get away for a while and had been driving the meandering country roads ever since. When he saw Fil stagger and then hit the pavement, what could he do but make sure she was okay?

He should never have put his arms around her, though. Huge, huge mistake. He could still smell the citrusy scent of her hair and feel its satin silkiness brushing his hands. His whole body still quivered with awareness of how comfortably she fit against him, all warm and soft and feminine.

And fragile.

In that split second he'd realized how hard he'd been on her, what she must be enduring from her own family. He might not agree with her choices, but who was he to sit in judgment? She needed a friend, perhaps now more than ever.

Filipa bounded down her porch steps and joined him at the car. "Sorry it took so long. The phone was ringing when I walked inside."

"Everything okay?" Nathan held the car door for her.

"Just Charlie saying he'd be working an extra shift flipping burgers at Cook Out." She slid into the passenger seat with a shiver. "Did I miss something about a front blowing in?"

"Don't ask me. I've been holed up with Mom all day learning how to run an equine therapy center." Nathan rounded the car and settled in behind the wheel.

As he pulled onto the road, Filipa asked, "So are you an expert now?"

Flicking a glance in her direction, Nathan smirked. "Not hardly. But come the end of October, I'll be running the place whether I'm ready or not."

"Is that when your mother officially moves to Texas?"

"Right. Tom's leaving tomorrow to check on his ranch, and Mom is staying here to help Kip and Sheridan kick off the fall class semester. Then Tom comes back so we can all celebrate Mom's birthday together before he spirits her off to her new life as a Texas ranch wife."

Filipa cocked her head. "I detect the slightest trace of resentment in your tone."

"Maybe." Yeah, he wanted Mom to be happy. Yeah, he

liked having Kip around as a brother-in-law. And yeah, he wanted to honor his dad's memory by ensuring Cross Roads Farm remained a successful and thriving operation.

But there'd been a few too many changes lately for Nathan's comfort level. Bottom line was he still missed his dad something fierce. And no matter how many times Kenneth Cross had reassured his son he was proud of him no matter what, Nathan could never quite shake the ridiculous idea that if only he'd taken horsemanship more seriously, Dad would have loved him even more.

The late-afternoon sky had turned a gloomy shade of gunmetal gray. The tires hummed over the well-worn asphalt, bouncing through potholes and vibrating across seams. The only other sound was Filipa's occasional sigh as she stared out the side window past meadows, woods, and farmhouses.

Recognizing a turnoff up ahead, Nathan aimed the car down a one-lane gravel road beneath a canopy of oaks, pines, and maples. At the end of the road they came upon a small lake with a strip of rocky shoreline. Nathan shifted into PARK and shut off the engine. "Remember this place?"

"We had my twelfth birthday picnic here. You pushed me in the lake with all my clothes on. It was barely sixty-five degrees that day, and I nearly froze before Mama got me home to change."

"Is *that* the way you remember it?" Nathan guffawed. "As I recall, you were chasing me with your *piñata* stick. I ducked behind a tree, but you couldn't turn fast enough, tripped over a log, and fell into the lake without any help from me at all."

Filipa crossed her arms and glared. "It was still your fault. If you hadn't kicked a hole in my *piñata* with your boot heel so you could get to the candy first, I'd have had no reason to be chasing you."

Those flashing brown eyes held Nathan's gaze, while his fingertips prickled with the urge to stroke the curve of her cheek. For a fleeting second he imagined what it would be like to erase her self-satisfied smirk with a long, lingering kiss.

Then he came to his senses. He didn't want this. *She* didn't want this. They were friends, that's all. Because once she came to *her* senses, he had no doubt she'd head back to New York and her music career lickety-split.

Which reminded him why he'd invited her on this drive. He wrapped both hands around the steering wheel and glanced toward the lake. "I said we needed to talk, didn't I?"

When he looked back at Filipa, the spark had left her eyes. She shifted, cradled her hands in her lap, picked at a fingernail. "If this is going to be a rehash of the other day—"

"Nope. This is an apology. I have no right to be telling you how to live your life. Heaven knows I'm still trying to figure mine out. I just want you to know I'm here as a friend. Any time. Any place."

She angled her head downward as her hand crept across the console to touch his sleeve. "Thank you."

The acquiescence in her tone nearly undid him. The urge to take her in his arms and kiss away all her troubles burned through him like wildfire. Never in his life had he wanted so much to be the big, strong hero, the knight in shining armor riding in on a white steed to rescue his damsel in distress.

With shaking fingers he reached for the ignition and started the car. "We should head back."

Chapter Five

What Filipa wouldn't give for a knight in shining armor to ride in and rescue her! Cleaning toilets was definitely *not* on her list of favorite activities.

Especially other people's toilets.

But Thanksgiving had come and gone, and she still had yet to find work she was qualified for *or* save up enough for a new set of wheels. When her mother suggested several weeks ago that Filipa might as well accompany her on some housecleaning jobs, how could she refuse? Money was money, right? And with clients all in a rush to have spotless houses for holiday company, Mama had been busier than ever.

"Are you finished in the bathroom yet?" Mama's voice rang from the adjoining bedroom. "I could use some help changing sheets."

"Be right there." Filipa flushed the toilet and dropped the lid, then set the plastic tote of cleaning supplies in the hallway before trudging into a bedroom suite the size of her parents' entire house. Wood floors gleamed beneath sunlight slanting through custom-made blinds. The lemony scent of furniture polish pricked Filipa's sinuses.

While Mama figured out which end was up on a set of king-size Egyptian-cotton sheets, Filipa smoothed out the mattress pad. She guessed the luxurious down-filled comforter piled at the foot of the bed cost more than what her mother earned in a week—and Mama cleaned three houses a day Monday through Saturday.

Backbreaking work. Often disgusting work. Yet Mama didn't complain.

"Hospital corners, Filipa. Don't forget."

"How could I, Mama? You taught me well." Filipa pinched the top sheet and blanket just so, folded them back together, and tucked in the tails. She straightened with a groan and eased her aching back.

Her mother stuffed a pillow into a sham while angling Filipa a knowing frown. "There are much easier ways to make a living, *mija*. Especially for someone with God-given talent and a fine education."

"Don't start with me, Mama." Nearly four months now, and the nagging continued. Would her parents never give up?

Who was she kidding? They were Beltrans!

They finished in the bedroom, gathered up their cleaning supplies, and tromped downstairs. After a final tidying up in the kitchen, Mama retrieved an envelope of cash from beneath the kitchen phone and counted out several bills into Filipa's hand.

"This is too much." Filipa tried to give half the money back to her mother. "You did most of the work."

"No, it's yours. The Deans are always generous at Christmastime. And you must save for a car. You will need a reliable one when you return—"

Filipa extended her hand, palm outward. "Can we go home now? I could use a long, hot soak in the tub."

"No time for that." Mama hurried her out the back door, set the alarm, and then locked the deadbolt behind them. "Tonight the Crosses hold their open house. You will help me in the kitchen."

How could Filipa have forgotten? The Christmas open house at Cross Roads Farm had become an annual tradition to honor and thank staff, clients, and volunteers. Filipa had missed the last several because of school and concert commitments, but she had fond memories of trailing Nathan through the festively decorated house, sampling the assortment of finger foods and desserts, and sipping Mrs. Cross's delicious homemade eggnog.

While Mama drove home, Filipa tilted her seat back in hopes of grabbing a catnap, but the fifteen-minute trip wasn't nearly long enough. She barely had time for a quick shower and a hastily made salami sandwich before dressing in the black skirt and white blouse Mama thrust at her.

"And pin up your hair," Mama ordered. "If you insist on doing the work of a maid, then you must dress like one."

Insist? Filipa most certainly did *not* intend to spend the rest of her days as a maid. Not that she saw her mother's work as lowly or undignified, but . . .

But what?

Papa lectured, Mama made her point more indirectly. The message remained the same: Neither would rest until Filipa returned to her music.

Sorry, Mama and Papa. I love you with all my heart, but that isn't going to happen.

Unfortunately, Filipa had absolutely no idea what she could possibly do instead. Secretarial work? She couldn't type worth a flip. Waiting tables? She did well to get her own plate of food to the dinner table without dropping it. Any other career worth consideration would require months or years of additional schooling and possibly professional certification.

"Filipa!" Mama pounded on the bathroom door. "We must go!"

"Coming, Mama." She poked the last hairpin into her bun and then dabbed her lips with pink frosted gloss. Her little sister's beaded Christmas-bulb necklace lay on a shelf above the toilet. Surely Elisa wouldn't mind if she borrowed it. After all, even the kitchen help was entitled to a sprinkling of Christmas cheer.

"Hey, how's my Pammy?" Nathan wrapped an arm around Pam Cardenas, the curly-haired adolescent who'd been a client at Cross Roads Farm for nearly five years now. "You look *mah*-velous, sweetie."

She answered with a shy giggle. "Are you going to be my helper ever again like you used to?"

"Sure hope so. I got to see you riding Radar a few times this fall. You're doing great!"

"I know." Tugging at the big red bow in her hair, Pam spun on her black patent toe and headed straight for the buffet table. Her mother cast Nathan a what-can-I-say? shrug before traipsing after her.

Nathan had to admit he missed working in the arena with the kids, all of them special in their own way. His only opportunities for the past few years had been filling in on Saturdays when he made it home for weekends. Since moving into the cottage the first of October and taking over management of the riding center, he'd had time for little else. Hopefully that would change once he grew more comfortable with his new responsibilities.

After a trip to the beverage table to refill his cup of hot spiced cider, Nathan wandered into the living room. It was pretty much wall-to-wall people by now, many faces he recognized and a few he didn't. He spotted Kip and Sheridan chatting with a couple near the fireplace and edged into the circle.

"Nathan, perfect timing." Sheridan smoothed a short blond curl behind her ear. "You remember Dave and Bev Williams, house parents from the group home?"

"How's it going?" Nathan nodded at Bev as he exchanged a hearty handshake with Dave.

"A good year so far—and most of the credit goes to your program." Dave slid his arm around his wife's waist.

Bev nodded in agreement. "I still can't get over what a difference we see in these kids' attitudes even after just one day out here with the horses."

Kip hooked his thumbs in the pockets of his dress jeans. "Sure wish Ryan could have come tonight. Grace has been asking about him."

"I remember Ryan." Nathan gave his brother-in-law a playful jab in the bicep. "A couple weeks after Mom assigned you as his helper, he was stuck to you like glue."

"Kip made quite an impression on him, that's for sure. He's a star student at the vocational college where he started this fall." Dave crunched on some sugared pecans. "We even talked Ryan into spending part of the Christmas holidays with his mother this year. They're actually able to communicate now without either one of them flying off the handle."

Nathan couldn't miss the subtle tensing in Kip's jaw. He was probably thinking about his own mother, still working hard to stay clean and sober but failing more often than not. How did Nathan and Sheridan get so lucky—no, *blessed* was the right word—to have had two such loving, devoted parents?

Sipping his cider, he glanced toward the dining room, where Filipa replenished a tray of hors d'oeuvres. When she'd arrived with her mother earlier, both of them dressed in caterers' attire, her gorgeous long hair twisted into a tight bun at her nape, he'd experienced a physical tightening in his gut. This was wrong . . . so wrong . . .

Not that Filipa shouldn't be helping her mother—she'd done so many times over the years, and none of them had thought anything of it.

But this was different. There was resignation in Filipa's posture, an emptiness behind her eyes. A mantle of hopelessness shrouded her like a dense, dreary fog.

"Nathan, are you listening?" Sheridan nudged his arm.

"Sorry, what?" He shook off his thoughts and tried to look interested in the conversation.

"Dave and Bev just mentioned they might have some suggestions for fundraising events—ideas that have proven very successful for the group home."

"That's great." Nathan no longer had to feign interest. "We're working to keep our tuition fees as low as possible, so I'm definitely looking into some kind of fundraiser for this spring."

"Then we should get together and talk—and the sooner, the better." Bev Williams set her empty plate and eggnog cup on a side table, fluttering hands reflecting her enthusiasm. "A big fundraising event takes *tons* of planning and organization. You've got to book a suitable facility, line up caterers, plan your entertainment, send out invitations, advertise—"

Already Nathan's head was spinning. He held up one hand. "I get the message! When are you free to meet with me and hash out some ideas?"

Dave whipped out his smartphone and began tapping away. "We've got some down time between Christmas and New Year's. Pick a day and we can meet at Kingsley Station for lunch."

After Sheridan double-checked her schedule, they agreed on a date and time. Nathan thanked the Williamses and then excused himself to visit with other guests. Pride welled in his chest as he shook hands with the grateful father of an autistic boy who'd hugged his parents for the first time ever following a riding class. Stories like Ryan's and that little boy's were among the biggest reasons Nathan's father had established the equine therapy center, and Nathan imagined how proud Dad would be to know his family was keeping the dream alive.

You're the face of Cross Roads Farm now, he could almost hear his father saying. *You'll do me proud, son. I know I can count on you.*

Nathan spent the next couple of hours glad-handing clients and volunteers and directing them to the buffet table for refreshments. His mouth felt frozen in a permanent smile, but he was growing to appreciate his role at Cross Roads Farm in ways he'd never expected. No longer just "Mrs. Cross's son, the business major," he was now CEO of a thriving family enterprise.

As he closed the front door behind one of their departing guests, his mother came up beside him. "This is our best turnout ever. Rosa and Filipa can hardly keep enough food on the table."

Nathan looped an arm around his mother's neck and squeezed, grateful Tom had brought her home to spend Christmas with her kids. "Admit it, Mom, you're going to miss all this now that you're a pampered Texas ranch baroness."

"Pampered? *Baroness?*" Nathan's mother swooped from beneath his arm and drove a finger into his sternum. "Why, you just wait. A year from now Tom and I might be running a brand new therapy center right there on the ranch."

"Knowing you, Mom, I don't doubt it for a second." With a booming laugh, Nathan whirled his mother around and aimed her back toward the living room.

They found several guests gathered around the piano, where Kip's little sister, Grace, attempted to plunk out a Christmas carol. Those around her harmonized the vocal parts, but the missed notes and slightly off-key singing made Nathan squint one eye in a barely concealed grimace.

His young friend Pam waltzed over and gripped his wrist. She stretched toward his ear and whispered. "That girl doesn't play very good. Can you play the piano?"

This time Nathan didn't bother hiding the pain in his expression. "Sorry, Pam, but I was the worst piano student ever. Just ask my mom."

His mother gave an exaggerated nod. "He's right."

"Then can Miss Sheridan do better?"

"Afraid not, kiddo." Nathan shared a knowing look with his mother, and they both stifled chuckles. The Cross kids must have been hiding behind the barn when God passed out the musical talent.

Then he glimpsed Filipa carrying a stack of empty

plates toward the kitchen. If anyone could coax sweet melodies from this musically challenged group . . .

He patted Pam's cheek. "Hold that thought, Pammy. I have an idea."

🐎

"We're out of decaf again." Filipa set the empty carafe on the counter.

Her mother glanced at the wall clock. "It isn't nine yet. Better brew another pot."

Filipa filled the reservoir with water and then measured beans into the grinder of the 12-cup automatic coffeemaker. Just as she flipped the switch, scratching and whining drew her attention to the laundry room door. She raised her voice above the whir of the grinder. "Be right back. I think Beau and Xena need to go out."

"Maybe you shouldn't—"

Her mother's warning came too late. The instant Filipa opened the door, an overweight chocolate Lab and a lumbering black Great Dane knocked her flat. Beau, the Lab, paused long enough to slather Filipa's face with his slobbery tongue, while Xena planted a giant paw in Filipa's midsection, forcing the breath from her lungs.

Seeing stars and gasping for air—not to mention nearly drowning in dog drool—Filipa lay still for a moment, taking inventory of her various body parts to make sure everything remained intact. When she opened her eyes, she found Nathan hovering over her and wearing an expression somewhere between a worried frown and a how-could-you-be-so-stupid grin.

"Lying down on the job, are we? How's the weather down there?"

"Slightly damp with occasional tsunamis." Filipa stretched one arm upward. "Give a girl a lift?"

"My pleasure." Nathan secured her wrist in his firm grasp and tugged her to her feet. "Except . . . we've got to stop meeting like this."

Warmth crept into her cheeks as she recalled the day she'd fallen in the road just as Nathan was driving by. Had it been that long since she'd seen him? Guess they'd both been rather preoccupied since then. Hitching a breath, she straightened her blouse and whisked at the dog hairs clinging to her skirt while Nathan let the dogs out the back door.

"I tried to stop her," Filipa's mother said as she set plates in the dishwasher. "But my daughter no longer listens to anything I try to tell her."

Filipa cast her eyes heavenward. *Lord, help me. I can't take much more of this.*

But she'd begun to suspect God wasn't listening anymore either.

Nathan cast her an empathetic glance. "You sure you're okay?"

She shrugged. "I should go wash up and fix my hair."

"I hear dog drool is the latest thing in wrinkle prevention." Nathan's eyes grew soft as he fingered a lock of hair that had pulled loose from her bun. "Anyway, I kind of like the messy look."

Filipa's nerves hummed beneath the whisper-like graze of his knuckles against her cheek. Edging away, she fumbled with bobby pins and strove for composure. "I really should—"

"Wait, Fil." Nathan's fingers closed around her forearm, freezing her to the spot. Something in his eyes made her heart stammer. He gave a low chuckle and tipped his head toward the door to the living room. "They could really use you in there."

Dirty plates? A spilled drink? More food? Freeing her arm, Filipa scraped clammy hands along her skirt, once again reminded that tonight she was the hired help. "Let me get a tray and I'll—"

"No, I meant—" Nathan now captured both her hands, his broad torso dwarfing her, his gaze so intense that she quickly averted her eyes. "I meant they need you to play for them."

A tiny designer horse emblem on his sweater riveted her attention. "Play?"

Sounds drifting from the living room finally registered —someone plunking notes on the piano, several off-key voices warbling the vocal parts. *Play. As in, accompany them on the piano.*

Filipa jerked away. She ducked around Nathan and started slamming dishes and empty trays on the center island. "Can't you see I'm busy in here? You're paying me for catering, not socializing with the guests."

"I think you've put in plenty of hours tonight already." Nathan forced her to set down the silver serving platter she was trying to scrape leftovers from.

"Please." She leveled her gaze at him, willing him to understand. "Don't."

Then her mother's hand landed on her shoulder from behind, tender but firm, her voice low and equally persuasive. "Do as he asks, *mija*."

Filipa squeezed her eyes shut, a physical sickness churning through her abdomen. She gulped air and prayed for control, hoping she could muster a civil response to their wheedling when every cell in her body wanted to scream at them to *leave her alone*!

Then Nathan came to her rescue—again. He circled the island and pulled her into his arms, the softness of his sweater combined with the musky-spicy scent of his aftershave like balm to her ragged emotions. "It's okay, Fil. It's okay."

Chapter Six

Nathan tossed another log into the potbelly stove and latched the door. A warm fire seemed the perfect antidote to a rainy end-of-December day. Christmas had come and gone. Mom and Tom had returned to Texas, Sheridan and Kip were getting settled in the big house, and Nathan was beginning to adjust to life in the caretaker's cottage.

Stretched out in an overstuffed chair, his feet resting on the ottoman, he switched on his laptop and prepared for another siege on the Cross Roads Farm financials. Later today he and Sheridan would meet with Dave and Bev Williams to discuss those fundraising ideas they'd mentioned at the Christmas open house.

Remembering that night, Nathan's thoughts shifted to Filipa. He could kick himself for his lame attempt to get her to play the piano. The tortured look in her eyes still haunted him.

As did the feel of her against his chest as he'd held her that night. He'd only meant to offer comfort, a brotherly hug of reassurance. But the way her head fit so neatly into the crook of his shoulder, the way her hands crept around his torso and clung to him like an anchor in a storm . . . he never wanted to let her go.

Get over it, man. You two are worlds apart. Or at least several hundred miles, once she called a halt to this so-called sabbatical and headed back to New York.

He'd barely pushed Filipa from his mind and delved into the business at hand when his cell phone "neighed," the horsey ringtone he'd assigned to calls from home—the number which now belonged to Kip and Sheridan, he kept reminding himself. He plucked his phone off the end table. "CEO Cross's office. How may I direct your call?"

"Very funny." Sheridan snorted a fake laugh. "Are you almost ready to head into town, little brother?"

"Give me five minutes. Who's driving, by the way?"

"You, of course. I'll be busy jotting down some thoughts for the meeting."

Ten minutes later they were on the road into Kingsley, windshield wipers flapping. Sheridan propped a steno pad on her knee while she chewed the cap of a ballpoint pen and stared out the windshield. "If this rain keeps up, we may have to take the long way home."

About that time, they reached the low-water crossing that often flooded during heavy rains. Nathan slowed the car. "Looks good so far. Maybe it won't get that bad."

A teasing tone in her voice, Sheridan said, "Well, if it does, we could always stop in at the Beltrans' on the way home. Fil sure has made herself scarce the last few months. At least we got to see a little of her at the Christmas party."

Something pricked Nathan's side—his conscience, no doubt. If he hadn't been so preoccupied with Filipa this morning, he'd have gotten a lot further along with his work. "She's probably been busy."

"Have you heard if she's any closer to finding a job?"

"Wouldn't know."

Sheridan shifted. "What's going on with you two anyway?"

Nathan felt her gaze boring through him. He swallowed and kept his eyes on the road. "Going on?"

"I thought sure you'd be spending a lot more time together now that you're both home. You used to be best friends, for crying out loud."

"We still are." *Sort of.*

"Well, best friends don't let friends spend the Christmas holidays alone."

Nathan steered around a pothole and then shot his sister a disbelieving sneer. "The Beltrans have five kids, in case you forgot. So I feel certain Fil hasn't lacked for company."

"I know. But with the way things have been between her and her parents since she left music school . . ."

As if he needed to be reminded. "I thought we were going to talk about fundraising ideas."

"Whatever you say." Sheridan flipped through the pages of her steno pad and made a couple of checkmarks. "But it wouldn't hurt to drop by and see her once in a while."

Yes, it would. In ways Sheridan would never understand.

At Kingsley Station they found Dave and Bev Williams waiting for them in the reception area, and a few minutes later a hostess seated them in a corner booth.

A ponytailed server in denim overalls and a red bandana took their orders. While they waited for their food to arrive, Bev pulled a three-ring binder from her satchel and opened it on the table between them. "Here's just a sampling of fundraisers held on behalf of Pine Valley Haven. We've done everything from personal appeals, to mass-mailing campaigns, to hundred-dollar-a-plate gala dinners."

Sheridan examined a brochure describing a charity golf tournament. "This looks interesting. I think we have a lot of parents who are golfers."

"Remember, the goal is to bring in dollars from outside sources." Dave squeezed a lemon into his water glass. "Otherwise, you're defeating the whole purpose."

"First and foremost," Bev explained, "you need to generate community interest and support. I'd suggest staging an event with the broadest possible appeal, something that not only sparks enthusiasm for what you're doing at Cross Roads Farm but also offers enjoyment and entertainment on a larger scale."

Nathan crossed his arms along the edge of the table. "Just how 'large' are we talking here?"

"I'm thinking . . ." Bev's eyes danced. "How about an evening of dinner and fabulous entertainment along with a live auction for several really, *really* fantastic items?"

"I'm liking this," Sheridan said, scribbling rapidly in her steno pad. "We get the parents and volunteers involved, have them mine their address books and business contacts for possible donors."

Dave slapped the table. "Exactly. And you'll need to recruit volunteers for the various committees—entertainment, dinner, ticket sales, donations—"

"Hold on." Nathan sat back, already feeling overwhelmed. "Cross Roads Farm isn't that big of an operation. I don't think we have the volunteer base to stage an event of this magnitude."

Bev's brow furrowed. "Not even including the clients' families and friends? I'm guessing you'd find more people willing to help than you imagine."

Her gaze turning thoughtful, Sheridan drew circles on the tabletop with her fingertip. "Nathan could be right.

Many of our parents and volunteers have day jobs, not to mention family and other commitments. We can't overburden them with a huge fundraising project."

"Okay, then, let's think smaller." Dave skewed his lips. "Something fun for the volunteers, clients, and their families but also a community draw."

Sheridan nibbled the end of her pen. "Something we could pull together with the fewest headaches for everyone involved."

A glimmer in her eye, Bev leaned forward. "What would you think of hosting a barbecue cook-off?"

Conversation instantly ceased, and Nathan could almost see the wheels turning in everyone's head while his own brain raced with the possibilities. Pitting the South's traditional pulled pork and chicken against Tom Jacobs's good ol' Texas-style beef brisket and sausage? Who could resist the challenge—or the menu?

He nodded slowly. "This could work."

"Great food, lively entertainment, family-friendly fun and games . . ." Sheridan grinned, enthusiasm lighting her face. "How long would it take to pull everything together?"

"A few months at minimum." Bev whipped out her smartphone and pressed some keys. "You'll want the best chance of nice weather, so I'd suggest late April or early May, before end-of-year school activities kick in."

Their meals arrived, and Nathan took advantage of the lull in conversation to let his brain hash through this jumble of ideas. Mom had tried to prepare him for the need to hold a fundraiser, but he never imagined that as soon as she left for Texas he'd be diving head first into completely uncharted waters.

Speaking of water, he noticed the trickling sounds on the restaurant's tin roof had swelled to a metallic drone.

Rain sheeted down the windows behind their table, obscuring his view of the train tracks beyond. Yep, they'd definitely need to take the long way back to the farm. He squeezed spicy brown mustard onto his burger bun and tried to steer his thoughts back to the fundraiser and away from Filipa.

"Yes, I understand. Thank you for your time." Filipa replaced the kitchen phone extension on its base and massaged the headache forming behind her eyes. Another job lead down the drain. She knew it would take some effort to find work she was qualified for and might even actually enjoy, but surely there must be someone hiring. After nearly four months of searching, she was ready to take anything that would get her out from under her parents' roof.

They'd have an easy answer for her: *Go back to New York.*

A roll of thunder shook the house. Hugging herself against the winter chill, Filipa paced to the front window and stared out at the pouring rain. The low-water crossing would surely be flooded by now. Poor Mama, exhausted from cleaning houses all day, would have to take the long way home. And Papa—Filipa pictured her father in soggy boots and a slicker as he darted back and forth bringing horses in from their pastures. No one worked harder or longer than Filipa's parents, and neither was getting any younger.

"Filipa, help!" Her little brother Joseph bounded into the room. "Elisa's gonna hit me!"

The sister in question stormed into the room, black

eyes blazing. "He scribbled all over my favorite book with a red marker!"

"All right, that's enough." Great, just great. While the kids were out of school for the holidays, Filipa (being conveniently unemployed) had been left in charge. She grabbed Joseph by his shirt collar and forced him to look at her. "Is this true, Joseph?"

He screwed up his face. "I only did it because she wouldn't let me play Clue with her and Naomi."

"He always loses the game pieces." Elisa huffed. "Besides, he cheats."

"I do not!"

"Okay, okay." Filipa sat them down on opposite ends of the sofa. "Until you two can play nicely together, you'll have to—"

Wailing sirens screamed. Filipa jerked her head toward the front window in time to see flashing lights streak past the house. Both kids clambered to their knees, leaning over the back of the sofa to peer out the window.

"Wow, they're in a hurry," Elisa murmured.

Seconds later Naomi darted into the room. "Was that an ambulance?"

"Yes, and a fire truck." Just one, though, so more likely a medical emergency rather than a fire, considering how hard as it was raining. Filipa palmed her abdomen, uneasiness churning. Only two properties lay between the Beltrans' and the low-water crossing: Cross Roads Farm and Emma Webber's place. Mrs. Webber must be in her eighties by now and lived alone. Maybe she'd suffered a stroke or heart attack. Filipa prayed they'd be able to help her in time.

She'd just diverted the kids' attention back to Joseph's misbehavior when the phone rang. Naomi snatched it up.

"Hello? . . . No, Mama isn't home." She blinked several times before passing the phone to Filipa. "It's Mr. Lorimer. He wants to talk to you."

Sheridan's husband? Filipa reached for the phone with trembling fingers. "Hello?"

"Filipa, it's Kip. Your dad's been hurt."

"Papa?" Her stomach heaved. "What—how?"

"I've got my hands full here, so long story short, he got nailed by Jet. The EMTs are seeing to him now, but you'll want to let your mother know and then meet them at the hospital."

Jet—the horse that hated thunderstorms. *Oh, Papa!* Hand pressed to her forehead, Filipa swallowed the bile rising in her throat. "The kids are all here, and I don't have a car."

About that time, the emergency vehicles sped by in the opposite direction, tires whizzing across wet pavement. All three kids stared at Filipa with frozen gazes, clearly sensing something was wrong. She tried her best to reassure them with a shaky smile.

Rustling sounds and muted conversation filled her ear, and then Kip spoke again. "Nathan and Sheridan just got back. I'll send them over. Sher can stay with the kids while Nathan takes you into town."

"Okay . . . Thank you." Breath snagging, Filipa clutched the phone to her chest and collapsed into the nearest chair. *Please, God, let Papa be all right—and let me be strong for the kids and Mama.*

Elisa approached with trembling lips and tucked her hands into Filipa's. "Is it Papa? I'm scared!"

Filipa pulled the curly-haired girl onto her lap. Seconds later both Naomi and Joseph had squeezed in close. She patted each of them in turn. "Papa had an accident, but I'm sure he'll be fine. Now please be calm and quiet while I phone Mama. She doesn't need to hear all of us blubbering. It'll only make her worry more."

As if Filipa wasn't worried enough for all of them!

The children gave her a little space while she keyed the speed-dial code for their mother's cell phone. Just as Mama picked up, Nathan and Sheridan appeared at the front door. Naomi let them in, and Sheridan immediately gathered the children around her on the sofa, offering hugs and gentle words while Filipa explained the situation to her mother and tried to keep her from panicking.

When she hung up, Nathan surrounded her with his strong arms. "He's gonna be fine, Fil, I promise." His hand crept up to cradle her head, while his warm lips found her forehead. "Come on, sweetie, get your coat and I'll drive you to the ER."

Only after they were miles down the road, with Filipa's heart beating harder and louder than the *whump-whump* of the windshield wipers, did that single word resonate: Nathan had called her *sweetie*. He couldn't have meant anything by it . . . could he? They were friends. Only friends.

Brushing an anxious tear from her cheek, she braved a glance in his direction. His steady gaze fixed on the road ahead, both hands fisting the steering wheel, jaw set with determination—everything about him spoke rock-solid strength, someone she could depend on, someone she could trust.

He caught her eye and smiled. "You doin' okay?"
She nodded. "Nathan?"
"Yeah?"
"Thank you."

Nathan steadied his hold on the cardboard tray before stepping off the elevator. The pungent aroma of freshly brewed coffee filled his nostrils as he found his way to the waiting room where he'd left Filipa and her mother.

He set the tray atop a stack of magazines. "No news yet?"

Rosa Beltran reached for one of the coffees, wrapping her fingers around the cup as if the heat could chase away the worry chilling her soul. "He is still in surgery. They say it may be a long while yet."

Nathan sat next to Filipa on a purple print sofa and tucked her hand into his. The thin, delicate fingers felt stiff and cold. He rubbed them gently. "He'll be fine. Hang in there."

She sniffed. "His knees were going bad anyway, and now one is completely shattered. They're going to try a knee replacement, but . . . what if he can never work again?"

Nathan had no reason to feel guilty, and yet he did. What in heaven's name was Manuelo doing out there with that horse, when everyone knew about Jet's fear of storms? Kip was the only one who'd ever managed to keep the horse calm. Several choice words paraded through Nathan's brain as he imagined giving Kip what-for for letting Manuelo anywhere near Jet this afternoon.

With a sigh, he handed Filipa a cup of coffee. "Your dad —all of you—you're like family. And the Crosses take care of family. The important thing now is getting your dad through the surgery and on the road to recovery."

Nodding, Filipa took a tentative sip from the cup and then rested her head against the back of the sofa. Her thick, dark lashes clumped in wet spikes. The slight tremor of her lips brought an ache to Nathan's chest.

The need to do something, to fix things somehow, overwhelmed him. He pushed to his feet. "I should call home." With a reassuring touch to Filipa's knee and a smile in her mother's direction, he started down the corridor in search of a quiet place to make the call.

A couple of rings later, Sheridan answered her cell. "I thought you'd never call. How's Manuelo?"

"Still in surgery. His knee's blown to smithereens. I have no idea if they'll be able to fix it." He palmed his brow, his next words as close to an angry shout as hospital courtesy would allow. "What was Kip thinking?"

"Don't blame Kip." Sheridan's tone bristled. "While we were enjoying a nice lunch with the Williamses, Lady colicked. Kip was tending to her all afternoon. The vet just left."

"Aw, man . . ." Heart sinking, Nathan paced to the window. "How is she?"

"Better. But Kip's exhausted, thanks for asking. And about ready to blow a gasket worrying about Manuelo."

"Sorry. I should have called sooner." In the background he heard the Beltran kids arguing over TV channels. "You doing okay with the kids?"

"They're fine. Charlie's home from work now, so I'm going to fix them all some supper and then probably walk home. I think the rain finally stopped." Sheridan's voice lost its edge. "How are Rosa and Fil holding up?"

"As well as can be expected." He explained Filipa's concern that her father would no longer be able to work. "I tried to reassure her, but . . ."

"I know. Call me when Manuelo is out of surgery. I

need to see what I can scrounge up to feed four hungry kids."

Nathan ended the call, then as he rounded the corner outside the surgical unit waiting area, the vitriol of raised voices assailed him. "What in the—"

Bursting into the room, he came upon Mrs. Beltran shaking her finger in Filipa's face. "This is your fault! I blame no one but you!"

"Mama, I'm sorry!" Tears streamed down Filipa's face.

A nurse in pink scrubs pushed her way between them. "Ladies, please! I know you're upset, but—"

"Of course I am upset! My husband nearly died in there!" Mrs. Beltran jutted her chin, rage crumpling her face into an ugly grimace.

"Hey, that's enough." Nathan set his hands on Filipa's shoulders and forced her to take two steps backward. "What's going on?"

Shivering, Filipa wrapped her arms around her ribcage. "Papa had a heart attack on the operating table. They almost lost him."

"Oh, no." Nathan pulled Filipa into his chest and then shifted his gaze to the nurse.

"He's in recovery. The staff cardiologist was called in immediately, and we have every reason to believe Mr. Beltran will pull through this just fine." The nurse slanted pointed looks at Mrs. Beltran and Filipa in turn. "But *only* if he has his family's full—and *calm*—support." With that, she excused herself.

"All right, you two. You heard the nurse." Nathan eased Filipa onto the sofa while Mrs. Beltran paced and seethed on the other side of the coffee table. He spied a box of tissues across the room and grabbed a handful for Filipa.

She blew her nose loudly. "Mama's right. This is my fault."

"How can you say that?" Nathan propped one hip on the sofa arm beside her. "It's the stupid horse's fault if it's anyone's."

"No." Mrs. Beltran halted in front of them, gray-streaked hair falling across flashing eyes. She swept it aside with an angry swipe. "If Filipa had stayed at music school where she belongs, her father would not have worried himself sick over her complete lack of regard for God's will."

Chapter Seven

Filipa stood in the barn doorway, hands on hips and her senses on overload with the smells of hay and horse manure —sweetly pungent smells that felt like home to her. The soft nickers of horses in their stalls, the rustle of shavings and straw, the clicks and thunks of hooves against feed buckets—*that* was the "music" she'd missed!

She gave a firm nod. "I can do this."

Now she just had to convince Nathan, Sheridan, and Kip.

And her parents.

The crunch of footsteps on gravel sounded behind her. She turned just as Nathan tugged at her ponytail, his face lighting in an ear-to-ear grin. "Fil, what are you doing over here so early? You should have knocked on my door."

She slid her hands into the deep, flannel-lined pockets of her father's corduroy barn coat, fingertips grazing ancient scraps of lint and hay. "I was enjoying how peaceful it is this time of day—the horses just waking up, dawn breaking in every shade of pink imaginable." She released a serene sigh, almost sorry Nathan had found her so soon.

Although she *had* come with a purpose in mind, a proposition she hoped he'd accept.

"It's nice, isn't it?" Dressed in jeans and mud-spattered boots, Nathan grabbed a halter and lead rope off the first stall door. "As long as you're here, want to help me take some horses out to pasture? Kip and I have been covering for your dad for now, but Kip's been laid low by a stomach bug."

"I'd be glad to help." Oh, boy, would she!

Nathan led a big brown horse out of the stall and handed Filipa the lead rope. "This is Sundown. He's been with us about three years now."

"Hi, fella." Filipa laughed as the horse graced her coat sleeve with a messy nose wipe that left a trail of slime behind.

"Let me grab another horse and we can walk them out together." From the next stall Nathan appeared with a sleek chestnut he introduced as "Radar." "These guys go in pasture four, up front."

They followed the lane past the caretaker's cottage, then between some pastureland and the main house. The brisk January morning brought a tingle to Filipa's cheeks and new hope to her heart.

As if catching the scent of fresh grass, Sundown whinnied and pranced. Filipa gave the lead rope a gentle tug and patted the horse's neck. "Easy, boy."

When Sundown lowered his head and settled into a less hurried walk, Nathan peered at Filipa over his horse's neck with an appreciative thrust of his jaw. "You're a natural at this."

She smiled back, her confidence growing. "Guess you could say I'm my father's daughter."

"How's he doing, by the way? We've been so busy here that I haven't had a chance to visit much."

"Strong enough to start getting feisty with the nursing staff. But they want to keep him in the hospital a few more days." They reached the gate to pasture four, led the horses through, and released them from their halters. As Nathan fastened the gate latch, Filipa mustered her courage. "Look, Nathan, I know my father's accident has left you in a bind, and I want to help."

"Thanks, Fil, but we'll manage. I placed an ad in the *Kingsley Sentinel* for a temporary stable hand—hiring subject to Sheridan's approval." He groaned as they started back toward the barn. "Naturally, she'll require a thorough background check."

"I wouldn't blame her." Filipa knew all too well the story of how as a child Sheridan had been traumatized by former employees who'd robbed the Crosses. Fortunately they were caught soon afterward and sent to jail. "But, um . . . I could save you the trouble and Sheridan the anxiety." Speeding up slightly, she swiveled on the heel of her hiking boot and danced backward in front of Nathan, beaming him her most persuasive grin. "Just hire me."

He stopped in his tracks, brow furrowed. "You serious?"

"As a—" She started to say "heart attack" but thought better of it. Chewing her lip, she scraped her toe across the dirt. "I can do this, Nathan. I *want*—no, the truth is I *need* to."

"But why, Fil? Shouldn't you . . ." He jammed his hands into the pockets of his hoodie. A muscle at the base of his jaw twitched. "I promised myself I'd quit nagging you about your music, but I can't help it. You have too much talent to be shoveling manure for a living."

She cocked a hip, hands fisted at her waist. "So shoveling manure is okay for somebody like my father but not okay for me?"

"You know what I meant." Nathan stared into the distance as if weighing his words. When he looked back at her, his expression was all business. "All right, here's my best offer, and you can take it or leave it. Half-days only, because this is a big job. Not that I think you can't handle the work, but face it, you haven't exactly been hauling tack or lifting hay bales since you went to New York."

No arguing there. Filipa crossed her arms. "Give me a couple of weeks and I'll be pulling my own weight. I'm stronger than I look. Any other conditions?"

"Be here by six every morning, rain or shine. Except at six a.m. there won't be much 'shine' for the next couple of months—if you last that long."

She glared.

"Okay, okay, just sayin'." Pinching her by the nape, Nathan spun her around and aimed her toward the barn. "Might as well get started teaching you the routine. The day has barely begun."

As she marched along with his hand squeezing her neck, a tiny shiver of anticipation rippled through her. Finally, she'd be doing something more satisfying than agonizing over broken guitar strings or rushing to pick up her concert formal from the dry cleaners or being chewed up and spit out by a merciless music instructor.

After leading the rest of the horses out to pasture, they set to work mucking stalls, spreading fresh shavings, and washing out water pails. Perspiration sliding down her ribs, Filipa soon had to toss her coat aside. The work was both exhausting and exhilarating.

"One thing I forgot to mention," Nathan said as he

showed her how to tear the right-sized flake off a hay bale. "Another condition of your employment is that you have to help with the Cross Roads Farm fundraiser."

Filipa scratched her nose. "Fundraiser?"

"Yes, ma'am." Nathan snatched a piece of straw from her hair and stuck it in his mouth, chewing on it like a country hick. Laying on a thick Southern drawl, he said, "Cross Roads Farm's gonna be sprucin' up for a rollickin' good time!"

A twinge of uncertainty crept up Filipa's spine. "What exactly would I be doing?"

"Well, little lady, I was thinkin' y'all might be jes' who we need to head up the entertainment committee."

She swiped the straw from between his teeth and then used it to poke him in the chest. "Well, you can just think again, Mr. Cross, because, number one, I know zilch about organizing a fundraiser. And number two, even if I did, I most assuredly would *not* volunteer to handle the entertainment."

"Come on, Fil." Nathan sighed and sank onto a hay bale, the humor leaving his eyes. "I only thought of you because I figured you'd have connections in the music world. At the very least, you could make sure we're getting quality entertainment at a reasonable cost."

He *had* to push the music issue. Filipa plopped onto the bale next to him. "It's not like I'm up on the local music scene. Any connections I have would all be back in New York."

His hand found hers, and he drew it into his lap. "Please, Fil, do this for me. Or if not for me, then for the farm. We need you."

Her gaze crept upward from their clasped hands to his face—the curve of his nose, the dimple in his chin, the full lips arching into a boyish smile that made her pulse scamper. "I don't know . . ."

He shifted his head slightly until their eyes met, and then, as his gaze slowly lowered to her mouth, she could feel every millimeter his eyes traveled like a physical touch. She watched him watching her lips and her world shifted. Everything . . . everything was about to change forever.

If you do this, it changes everything.

Nathan hovered so close that he could taste the quick, warm breaths pulsing between Filipa's parted lips. Sweet. Entrancing. Deliciously tempting. Did he dare risk it, risk ruining a nearly lifelong friendship with a game-changer of a kiss that clearly they both desired?

Because judging from the look in Filipa's eyes, she was feeling this, too—whatever "this" was.

Then suddenly the look was gone. Filipa's glance jerked past Nathan's shoulder, and she popped off the hay bale like a jack-in-the-box. "Sheridan!"

Nathan whipped his head around to find his sister silhouetted in the open door. He rose to his feet and stuffed clammy hands into his pockets.

"Hey, guys. Didn't expect to find you here, Fil." Sheridan strode toward them, a puzzled look on her face. "Am I interrupting something?"

Filipa rocked on her heels. "Nathan was just showing me my new barn duties."

"Y–yeah." Nathan cleared the nervous waver from his throat. "Fil's going to help fill in for her dad for the time being."

"Oh, really?" Sheridan's brows climbed into her wispy blond bangs.

"I needed a job anyway," Filipa said. "And I love it here, always have."

Noticing Filipa start to shiver, Nathan found her coat and draped it across her shoulders. "See, I was thinking with Fil here in the mornings and Grace helping out when she comes home from school, we don't have to worry about interviewing temporary help until we know when and if Manuelo will be able to return to work."

Sheridan nodded. "Good thinking, Mr. CEO. I like your style." Her lips slanted in a crooked grin. "Well, carry on, you two. Don't let me interrupt this, um, training session."

With a quick backward glance and a wink that said she'd seen way more than she should have, Sheridan marched out of the barn.

Nathan huffed out a sigh and turned toward Filipa. "About earlier—"

"If we're finished for now, I should head home and clean up so I can go visit my dad." She slid her arms into her coat sleeves. "I'll be back first thing tomorrow, six a.m. sharp."

Back to business as usual. Considering all the lectures Nathan had given himself about *not* getting romantically involved with Filipa, why was he so disappointed? He followed her out to her father's dirt-encrusted blue pickup. She clambered into the driver's seat and then turned a wistful glance his way. Was she sorry, too?

He leaned into the open door, reluctant to let her leave. "You'll think about the fundraiser thing, right? I'm counting on you."

A growling noise ripped from her throat as she aimed a

pleading gaze heavenward, but an acquiescent smile twisted her lips. "Okay, okay!"

As Nathan watched her drive away, he couldn't keep the silly grin off his face. Yep, he'd just maneuvered things so he and Fil would be spending more time together—a *lot* more time together, if he had his way. A bounce in his step, he returned to the cottage. Time to fire up the laptop and get some work done. With volunteer training for the spring semester just two days away, classes beginning next Tuesday afternoon, and a fundraising barbecue cook-off in the works, life was about to get a whole lot busier.

Rinsing her hair under the pulsing shower stream, Filipa pondered her recent change of circumstances. More than just landing a job or agreeing to help—make that *consider helping*—with this Cross Roads Farm fundraiser Nathan had just sprung on her, she found herself feeling optimistic about the future for the first time since coming home from New York.

As for that almost-kiss . . . a tremor snaked through her at the memory. When Sheridan interrupted them, Filipa had been relieved, and maybe a teensy bit annoyed. Though she hadn't seen all that much of Nathan since coming home last summer, each time they were together, the romantic twinges he stirred in her had only grown stronger, no matter how hard she'd tried to suppress them. But now that he was both her best friend *and* her employer, no sense confusing their relationship any more than it already was.

After drying her hair, dabbing on some makeup, and dressing in slacks and a bright fuchsia sweater, she climbed back into her father's pickup and headed into town. She could really use a sturdier pair of boots and some thicker socks before reporting for work in the morning. Afterward, she'd have just enough time to visit Papa at the hospital before the bus dropped the younger kids off after school.

The farm supply store stocked exactly what Filipa needed in comfy padded socks and zip-up, waterproof paddock boots. She paid for her purchases with money saved from helping her mother clean houses, then stopped for a salad lunch at Kingsley Station before driving to the regional hospital on the outskirts of Charlotte.

When she reached her father's room, she found him propped up in bed with his Bible in his lap and reading glasses perched on the end of his nose. His smile of welcome eased the anxiety she'd built up during the drive to the city. "My Filipa. Come give your papa a hug."

"How are you feeling today?" Careful not to jar his heavily bandaged knee, she eased onto the side of the bed and pressed her cheek to his.

"Tired, but better." As he laid his glasses atop his open Bible, his chest rose and fell on a deep sigh. "Lying in this bed has given me much time to think . . . and to pray."

Filipa angled her father a twisted smile. "Still praying I'll come to my senses?"

He chuckled. "No, *mija*, I pray that I will come to mine." At her confused stare, he continued, "After learning how close I came to death, I realized I would have gone to meet my Lord with far too many regrets."

"Oh, Papa, God knows what a good man you are. What could you possibly have to regret?"

He lowered his gaze to her left hand, then turned it over to stroke the fading calluses on each fingertip with a gentleness that made Filipa's breath freeze in her throat. "More than anything, I regret the sadness I have caused my eldest child because I did not trust her to choose her own path."

"You only wanted what was best for me."

"*Sí*. But as you have said many times, you are not a child any longer. I have been wrong to withhold my approval on the condition that you bend your will to mine."

To hear her father speak so, to see the look of contrition in his eyes, brought a knot to Filipa's chest. She laid her head against his shoulder. "Thank you, Papa. Thank you for understanding."

He patted her back in a gently soothing rhythm. "I do not say I understand. But I relinquish my will to the Father's. If the Lord desires that you return to your music, I trust He will kindle that flame anew when it suits His heavenly purposes."

Don't count on it, she wanted to say. Instead, she planted a grateful kiss on her father's cheek and then straightened. "I do have some good news this morning. I've found a job."

Papa cast her a dubious frown. Obviously, this was not the news he wanted to hear. "Where will you be working?"

"At Cross Roads Farm." Filipa described her agreement with Nathan. "It's perfect, don't you see? I'll be saving your job for you until you're able to work again, and in the meantime I'll have my afternoons free to continue looking for something permanent."

Not that she expected to find anything more satisfying than working outdoors and spending time with horses. Even after Papa was on his feet again, both his heart condition and his new knee would require a lengthy period of rehabilitation before he could handle his full workload. Filipa might be able to plan on many more weeks if not months of working at Cross Roads Farm.

Unwittingly, her thoughts jerked back to those

moments in the barn that morning . . . Nathan's face hovering inches from hers, his eyes dreamy, lips parted, one hand inching toward her face.

She blinked rapidly and drew a quick breath. Working for Nathan Cross could well turn out to be an even more pivotal decision than leaving music school.

While all these thoughts paraded through her mind, Papa toyed with his reading glasses and chewed his lip. Finally he lifted his eyes to meet hers. "I am thankful to have such a dutiful daughter willing to work so hard to ensure her family's livelihood. But I cannot deny it saddens me. I do not like to think of my beautiful, talented Filipa toiling in such conditions when—" He glanced away, jaw muscles bunching. "No, I will not speak so again. Go, my daughter. Find your own way. And may the Lord be with you."

Filipa's throat ached with the love she felt for this man. His stubbornness, his pride, his determination to ensure his children's futures—it all paled beneath his unswerving devotion to the Lord and to his family. She prayed for even a portion of such faith and strength of character in her own life.

Chapter Eight

January had drawn to a close, taking with it the worst of the winter weather. Or so Filipa hoped. It hadn't been a particularly harsh winter for this part of North Carolina, but Filipa hadn't considered how cold it could feel at six in the morning with a drizzly rain falling and a chilly northerly wind nipping at her cheeks.

And, like the proverbial postman, neither rain nor snow nor sleet nor gloom of night must keep this stable hand from her appointed rounds.

She tugged her stocking cap lower around her forehead and ears before trundling a cartload of soiled shavings and horse manure out to the collection bin. As she came even with the garage, Beau and Xena bounded up to greet her. With yips and tail wags, the big dogs pranced in circles around Filipa and the manure cart.

"Hey, guys. Glad to see you, too." Laughing through what had become a morning ritual, Filipa yanked off one of her gloves to give the Lab and Dane proper scratches behind the ears. "Now let me get back to work, will you? It's cold out here!"

"There's hot chocolate inside when you're done."

She spun around to find Kip approaching from behind. "Sounds wonderful—thanks!"

He adjusted his tan felt Stetson and nodded toward the cart. "Looks like a full load there. You got it okay?"

"Under control." Filipa worked her hand back into her glove and then gripped the cart handles.

"All righty, then. Say hi to your dad for me." Kip shot her a parting grin as he headed toward the barn.

Giving the cart a shove, Filipa could only shake her head. That had to be one of the longest conversations she'd had with the laconic cowboy. She hoped he was a little more talkative with his wife, or else Sheridan must be enduring some really boring evenings.

Nathan, on the other hand, kept Filipa entertained for hours with his wit and charm. At least when she gave him the chance. Lately, however, she'd been concentrating extra-hard on keeping their relationship strictly business. She'd been savoring the serenity of her work here far too much to jeopardize it by risking another almost-intimate moment like they'd experienced a few weeks ago.

Returning to the barn with the empty cart, she parked it in front of the next stall to clean. Another load of manure, another bag of shavings spread, feed and water buckets hosed out and refilled, fresh hay deposited in each stall, and she was finished. Anticipating the sensation of hot chocolate warming her insides, she dusted off her gloves and marched toward the house.

Sheridan opened the back door wide. "'Morning, Fil. Come on in."

"Kip mentioned you were offering hot chocolate to warm up a half-frozen stable hand?"

"Sure am." Sheridan swiveled a rack of single-serving

beverage pods. "We've got dark chocolate, chocolate mocha, white chocolate, mint chocolate latte—name your poison."

"Chocolate mocha sounds fabulous." Filipa kicked off her boots and left them on a mat by the door. She stuffed her gloves and stocking cap into the pockets of her coat before hanging it on a hook.

Sheridan set a mug under the spout and then started the brewer. "Do you have a few minutes to talk about the barbecue cook-off?"

A twinge of anxiety stiffened Filipa's spine. Up to now, she'd been able to deflect most attempts to draw her into involvement with the Cross Roads Farm fundraising plans. It had been a busy month, what with mastering her new job requirements, shuttling Papa back and forth to his physical therapy and cardiac rehab appointments, and generally being as much help as possible to ease Mama's burden. But now that chores were going more smoothly and she'd settled into a comfortable routine, she was running low on excuses.

With a burble and a hiss, the brewer signaled the beverage was ready. Sheridan placed the mug in front of Filipa and took the chair cater-cornered from hers. "Plans are really shaping up," she said. "Several of the parents and class volunteers are already getting involved. One of our parents owns a printing firm in Waxhaw and has offered to do mailings and posters."

"That's great." Filipa traced a whorl in the wood-grained tabletop with one stubby fingernail. "To be honest, I'm not sure why Nathan thought I could help. I really don't know much about this sort of thing."

Sheridan tossed out a light laugh. "Join the crowd! This is a learning experience for Nathan and me, too." Growing serious, she stretched a hand across the table to touch

Filipa's arm. "Look, I know Nathan tapped you for helping find entertainment, but if you're not comfortable with that, there are plenty of other things you can do."

Filipa blew upon the surface of her cocoa before taking a careful sip. She kept her eyes averted. "Like I told Nathan, I'm not exactly connected with the local music scene."

"Don't worry about it." Bouncing up from her chair, Sheridan retrieved a thick manila folder from the counter and fanned the contents out on the table between them. "For now, maybe you could let me pick your brain about a few things. I'm going so cross-eyed over this project that I could really use some objective feedback."

Giving a shrug, Filipa angled her chair for a better look at Sheridan's notes. For the next hour they pored over publicity venues, event supplier price lists, and flyers from other barbecue cook-off events, while tossing out ideas about entry fees, prizes, and possible corporate sponsorships.

Finally Sheridan heaved a sigh and shoved her chair back. "Thanks, Fil. You've really helped me regain some perspective. If we're not careful, this thing could easily explode into way more than we can handle."

The back door creaked open, and Nathan poked his head through the opening. "Is this strictly a hen party, or can I come in?"

Sheridan winked at Filipa. "Always room for a rooster, as long as you keep the crowing to a minimum."

Dressed in slim-fitting jeans and a red North Carolina State sweatshirt, Nathan plopped into the chair next to Filipa's. He tweaked a strand of her hair. "When I saw your pickup still parked outside, I figured you two must be in here having a gabfest."

Filipa tried to keep from hunching her shoulders at the

sudden quiver his nearness elicited. "As a matter of fact, we've been talking business."

"Goodness, will you look at the time!" Pushing to her feet, Sheridan crammed all her notes into the folder. "I've got tons yet to do before classes this afternoon. See y'all later!"

Mouth agape, Filipa stared as her friend bolted from the kitchen faster than a racehorse out of the starting gate. It didn't take a PhD to figure out Sheridan had purposely left Filipa alone with Nathan. Swallowing, she slanted him an uneasy glance. "Guess I should be going, too." She started to rise.

"Not yet." Shifting, he planted one foot behind the leg of her chair to keep her from pushing away from the table. He trapped her hand in both of his.

"Nathan—" The walls of her throat thickened. She didn't dare meet the gaze she could feel boring through her temple.

"Hold still, will you? There's this . . ." One hand rose toward her neck. Fingertips like a flame against her skin, he eased the hair off her nape. From the corner of her eye she glimpsed a quick flick of his wrist. "Got it!"

"Got *what*?" she squeaked as he sprang from his chair and flushed something down the garbage disposal.

He chuckled and dispensed a blob of hand-washing foam into his palm. "You probably don't want to know."

Suddenly itching all over, she rose so quickly that she nearly tipped over her chair. She scrubbed her neck with one hand and combed anxious fingers through her hair with the other. "What was it? A tick? A spider? *What*?"

"Ah, the perils of working in a barn." Nathan rinsed and dried his hands. When he turned to face her, his eyes twinkled with a teasing grin.

Filipa's face warmed. And to think, seconds ago she'd worried Nathan was about to try to kiss her again. Well, maybe not worried, so much as . . .

His grin mellowed into a crooked smile. Half-lidded eyes obscured the playful twinkle of moments ago. Hands still slightly damp with the scent of melons clinging to them, he cupped Filipa's chin.

She drew in a tiny, soundless breath, unable to think, unable to move, unable to keep this from happening even if she wanted to. "Nathan . . ."

His gaze searched hers. "Tell me to stop if you don't want this as badly as I do."

Unable to deny the longing that swelled her heart, she remained silent, a painful swallow coursing down her throat.

Slowly, tenderly, his mouth lowered upon hers, searing her lips like a brand. His hands moved from her face to her shoulders, then slid around her back to pull her even closer, all the while his kiss growing more insistent.

Shivering, Filipa feared her knees would give way. She returned the kiss with a fervor she didn't know she possessed, her hands caressing his neck, twining in the thick, dark curls at his nape.

And then reality set in. She broke away with a violent shove, her breathing ragged. "Stop, Nathan." Her voice was little more than a rasp. "We have to stop."

Stop? When everything within him ached for more? It took Nathan a full minute before he could think rationally again. Turning aside, he pressed his palms into his eye sockets. "I never meant to take advantage, Fil. I thought . . . I thought you wanted this, too."

Her panting breaths continued. She strode past him and lifted her coat from the hook. With one hand on the doorknob, she lowered her head. "I don't know . . . maybe on some level I did. But it can't happen again. Ever."

He sighed, feeling like the floor had been ripped out from under him. "Why, Fil? Why can't it?"

Her only reply was a brisk shake of her head before the door whispered shut behind her.

Stupid, stupid, stupid! Nathan hammered the countertop with his fist, then banged a few cupboard doors for good measure. He was about to kick an empty dog dish across the room when Kip stepped through the back door.

"Whoa! What's got your dander up?"

Self-loathing tore through Nathan's throat in a growl. He clawed his temples. "I think I just ruined a beautiful friendship."

"You mean Filipa?" Kip snorted as he rested his Stetson on a hook. He shrugged out of his fleece-lined denim jacket. "She did look mighty unhappy when she drove away just now. What'd you say to her?"

"It's not what I said. It's what I *did*." Nathan snatched a glass from the cupboard, filled it from the fridge water dispenser, and gulped the liquid down in three gigantic swigs. But one glass of ice water wasn't nearly enough to cool the fire raging inside him.

Kip pulled out a chair and sat down to kick off his boots. Wiggling his toes against the dirt-stained ends of white tube socks, he leaned back and finger-combed his hair. A sweat ring matching the inside of a riding helmet suggested he'd just finished his regular training ride on Jet. "Okay, I'm listening. What'd you do exactly that has Filipa so upset? I sure hope you didn't fire her, because she works harder than just about anybody on the farm."

"No, I didn't fire her. But she just may quit after this." Nathan flipped a chair around and straddled it, chin resting on his folded arms. A low moan rattled his chest. "I kissed her."

"You . . . kissed her." Kip drew a hand down his face, his gaze slithering sideways in a look of confusion. "Yeah, I can see why that would just break her pea-pickin' heart."

Why Nathan thought his taciturn brother-in-law would understand, he had no idea. But the guy had won Sheridan's love, hadn't he? He must have *some* insider knowledge about romance. "Help me out here, man. How do I fix this?"

"Buddy, you're askin' the wrong guy."

Nathan snickered out a humorless laugh. "In case you haven't noticed, bro, you're the only other *guy* on the place these days."

Elbows poking out, Kip braced his hands on his thighs. He frowned as if this whole subject pained him to no end. "Okay, let's back up a few steps. Did you mean to kiss her?"

"Uh, yeah." Nathan's tone indicated his answer was a no-brainer.

"Was she, uh . . . receptive?"

"Definitely." At least at first.

Kip's eyes narrowed in an accusing glare. "So then you went a little further, and she—"

"No!" Nathan exploded to his feet. "No way, man! It wasn't like that." He spun around and braced his palms against the cold tile edge of the island. Dropping his volume several decibels, he murmured, "Not that I didn't want to. Heaven help me, I think I'm falling in love with that girl."

Groaning, Kip pushed to his feet. He propped his hips

against the island, arms crossed. "I may be a little slow catchin' up here, but sounds like Filipa doesn't exactly return your affection."

"Not romantically, anyway. Now I don't know how we'll ever go back to being just friends."

Several minutes of silence fell between them, while Nathan continued to berate himself for following his heart instead of his head. Hadn't he been telling himself for months that a relationship between them could never work? Besides, it didn't take rocket science to figure out Fil had pleaded for this stable hand job because it seemed the perfect opportunity to dodge whatever demons had driven her away from music.

But every morning since she'd begun filling in for her dad, Nathan had found himself drawn to the window to watch her at work. He'd memorized her swaying walk as she led horses out to pasture. He'd learned the subtle flex of her shoulders as she trundled the manure cart back and forth between the barn and the collection bin. He'd fretted over her furrowed brow when the manure cart got stuck in a rut, celebrated her happy grin when a horse nuzzled her cheek, savored every nuance of her changing expression for the deeper insight it offered into the woman he could no longer think of as "just" a friend.

Finally Kip released a noisy sigh. "There's only one piece of advice I can offer, and this comes straight from personal experience. You can run from your problems, but you can't hide, because whatever you're running from always has a way of catching up to you when you least expect it."

Nathan hiked his chin. "Is that little gem meant for me, or for Fil?"

"Both of you, I s'pose." Kip pushed off the island and

hooked his thumbs in his belt loops. "Bottom line is you have to be honest. With yourself and with her. Talkin' to me isn't doing you a lick of good."

Eyes narrowed, Nathan poked his brother-in-law's bicep. "You're smarter than you look, cowboy."

Kip grinned and slugged him back. "And you're dumber'n a doorpost if you let a sweet little filly like Filipa get away."

Filipa propped a shoulder against the doorframe between the kitchen and living room. "What sounds good for lunch, Papa? Soup again? A grilled cheese sandwich?"

"Either is fine." Her father adjusted the cold pack wrapped around his knee and then signaled her over. "But first, sit with me for a few minutes, *mija*."

Lips pursed, Filipa trudged across the room and plopped onto the arm of his recliner. Looping an elbow around his neck, she kissed the edge of his receding hairline. "You're sick and tired of convalescing, aren't you, Papa?"

"That is true. However . . ." He cocked his head to shoot her a one-eyed glare. "What sickens me even more is the frown I constantly see on my daughter's face. At first you seemed so happy to work at the farm. But this past week, not so much." A glint of hopefulness brightened his gaze. "Perhaps you have experienced a change of heart?"

"No, Papa." At least not in the way her father implied. She shifted to stretch one leg alongside his on the footrest. "Things have gotten a little . . . tense . . . between Nathan and me."

"He is not managing the farm as well as his mother?"

"No, he's doing a great job."

"He is making you work too hard?"

"Are you kidding? He's bent over backward to make sure I don't take on more than I can handle."

"Ah. Then it must be that you are falling in love."

Filipa scrambled to her feet in a huff. "I think I'd better start lunch."

In the kitchen she slammed pans and utensils and cans of soup as if the cacophony could drown out the thoughts she'd been doing her best to avoid since that . . . that . . .

Oh, mercy, that kiss!

Why now, of all times? She simply wasn't ready for a relationship. Not with Nathan, not with anyone. Yes, she'd fantasized about falling in love. Even convinced herself that once she'd closed the door on a music career, she'd finally have time for romance.

But not yet. Not until she figured out where her life was headed. Common sense told her she couldn't plan on making a living as a stable hand indefinitely. Until she'd walked in her father's footsteps both figuratively and literally, she hadn't fully comprehended how physically demanding the work was.

Not to mention the typical hay bale weighed almost as much as she did.

Emptying a can of chicken barley soup into a pan, Filipa heaved a groan. Life was supposed to get simpler once she left music school. Her plans—assuming she even had plans—kept getting turned on their heads, and now everything seemed more complicated than ever.

Nathan, Nathan, why did you have to kiss me?

And why, oh why, couldn't she stop thinking about it?

"Fil, we have to talk."

"Can't you see I'm busy?" Breathing hard, Filipa heaved another pitchfork full of soiled shavings into the manure cart. One more stall and she'd be finished.

Nathan marched through the stall door and ripped the pitchfork from her hands. "That manure isn't going anywhere. And neither are you until you sit down and talk to me about what happened last week."

Thrusting her hands into her pockets, she stared at the ground. "What happened was a mistake. I've already forgotten about it."

"I don't think so." Nathan stepped closer, planting the pitchfork tines into the hard-packed earth beneath the shavings. "Because if you had, you wouldn't be avoiding me like you have been ever since."

She squeezed her eyes shut and cursed the racing heart beneath her breastbone that proved Nathan's words true. Turning a pleading gaze upon him, she murmured, "Can't we go back to the way things were?"

"How do you propose we do that?"

"I don't know." She shrugged. "I just know we have to if I'm going to keep my sanity."

"What about *my* sanity?" He extended his hand toward her but snatched it back when she flinched. "I kissed you, Fil. I kissed you because I'd been wanting to practically since I first ran into you at the wedding. And you responded. Don't tell me you didn't."

She'd lied once to him already this morning. She wouldn't lie again. A shuddering breath shook her. "You took me by surprise. I was caught up in the moment."

"Yeah, and the surprise was you discovered you're starting to have feelings for me."

"Yes—no—oh, just stop it, Nathan!" Filipa yanked the

pitchfork out of the dirt, and Nathan had to duck out of the way when she resumed shoveling manure with ferocity.

Nathan's voice rose above the scrape of the pitchfork and her labored breathing. "You can fill a hundred carts with manure, but it won't make this go away."

She halted, spent. Perspiration soaked her temples and poured down the inside of her sweatshirt. Slowly she turned to face him. "You want to talk? Let's talk. Let's talk about the fact that you're a white-bread rich kid and I'm a Latina daughter of immigrants."

A stunned laugh burst from Nathan's lips. "Where did *that* come from? We practically grew up together, and now you're pulling the ethnicity card on me? And, please—*rich kid*? I'll be paying off student loans into the next millennium."

Fatigue and shame drove Filipa to the nearest hay bale, where she sank in a heap of despair. She didn't dare look up when Nathan plopped down beside her, but she didn't resist when he wrapped one arm around her and pulled her close.

"I'm sorry, Nathan." She shivered out a sigh. "I've been in a very bad place emotionally since I came home from New York. Then my father's accident, and now this . . . *thing* between us . . ." She nuzzled deeper into the crook of his shoulder, the softness of his fleece jacket cushioning her cheek. "Please, just be my friend again."

"I never stopped." His lips pressed her temple, but there was no passion in this kiss, only sympathy and understanding. And maybe a touch of forgiveness. "I'm here for you—as a friend—no matter what. And I'll give you all the space you need to figure things out."

"Thank you." The words came out in a whispered exhalation. She sat up and tucked a stray lock of hair behind her ear. "I should get back to work so I can finish in time for Papa's PT appointment this afternoon."

Nathan gripped her forearm, preventing her from rising. "One question and I won't ask again. Is there *anything* you're not telling me about why you left music school?"

Filipa knew from Nathan's probing stare exactly what he meant. She bent forward, images racing through her brain. The bearded instructor who liked sitting hip-to-hip with her on the piano bench and couldn't quite keep his hands on the ivories. The first-year guitar student she'd tutored who one day cornered her against the door and declared his undying love while breathing hot and heavy on her neck. The first-chair oboist with whom she'd shared a ride to a concert, only to have him take a "wrong turn" down a deserted road. When he tried to ply her with the cheap wine he'd already been tippling, she swiped his keys and then called the cops while hiking back to the main road.

Oh, yes, Filipa had fended off a few inappropriate advances in her time, not all that unusual in the music and entertainment industry, according to some people. But honestly—and unfortunately—sexual harassment remained a real possibility no matter what career path a woman chose.

She wove her fingers through Nathan's and squeezed. "It's nothing like what you're thinking."

"So . . . your feelings about the kiss . . . about me . . ."

His boyish insecurity tugged at her heart. More than anything, she wished she could give him the answer he wanted, but both her feelings and her future remained far too unsettled. Releasing his hand, she tucked her own beneath her arms as she rose. A few steps away, she turned to face him. "I promise you, Nathan, the only thing coming between us is *me*. It isn't you. It isn't anything that happened to me at school." One shoulder hiking, she cast Nathan a helpless frown. "I wish I could give you a reason that made sense, but how can I explain something I don't fully understand, myself?"

Chapter Nine

"Okay, this is a good start." Nathan stepped back from the whiteboard and tapped the capped end of a red marker against his chin. "We already have three barbecue teams signed up, and we've got at least two corporate sponsors on the hook."

"I have more news along those lines." Sheridan glanced around the Sunday-school room at Kingsley Faith Fellowship, where their planning team had been meeting every week since mid-January. "Kingsley Station has offered to supply all the disposable plates, utensils, napkins, and cups. They'll also provide sweet tea and lemonade."

Nathan added the information to the sponsor column on the whiteboard. "It sure would help the bottom line if we could get table and chair rental donated." He looked to Peggy Abbott, who'd been a Cross Roads Farm volunteer since the program began. "What are the chances, Peg?"

"I'm working on it, but my contact at the rental company is stonewalling." Peggy keyed something into her tablet. "I just forwarded you a copy of his latest email."

"Thanks. Let's hope he comes through." Nathan

reviewed his agenda. Only one item remained: entertainment. He puffed out his cheeks in an explosion of air and tried to steer his thoughts away from the woman whose expertise could have added so much to this discussion.

But Filipa had made it perfectly clear she wouldn't be attending any meetings. Nathan couldn't argue with her reasons—early mornings working at the farm, driving her father to appointments several times a week, seeing to the younger kids after school, taking over the household chores her hardworking mother usually came home to. Reasons that, on the surface, seemed honorable and altruistic, the dutiful daughter doing all she could to ease her family's burden.

Nathan suspected a much deeper motivation, however, and it all came down to guilt.

Something bumped Nathan's ankle—Sheridan kicking him under the table. Her raised-brow smile gave a clear signal he needed to quit lollygagging and get on with the meeting.

"Oooookay," he said, shifting in his chair. "Let's move on to live entertainment. I've contacted a couple of possibilities, including the band that played at my mom and sister's wedding reception last summer, but these guys get booked up months in advance. Anybody want to throw out some other ideas?"

Hemming and hawing followed, until Karen Cardenas, Pam's mother, spoke up. "My cousin's in an amateur bluegrass band. They're pretty good, not to mention cheap."

"Cheap, as in free?" Nathan jotted a note on his legal pad.

Karen chuckled. "The lure of a captive audience and guaranteed publicity goes a long way."

Nathan shared a look with Sheridan, who apparently read his concern. She turned to Karen and asked, "Are they performing anywhere that we could get a preview?"

"Give me a sec and I'll find out." Karen excused herself to make a call.

While she was out of the room, Nathan confirmed plans for the group's next meeting. They were a small but dedicated group, only a few with actual fundraising experience but all with big hearts for Cross Roads Farm and willing to put in the work to make this event a success. While Nathan waited for Karen Cardenas to return, he sent up a prayer of gratitude, because he sure couldn't do this job without each and every one of them.

Karen returned and slid a piece of scratch paper across the table to Nathan. "Here's their next gig, three nights at Darlene's Country Diner over in Pineville starting this Friday."

"Great. Anybody who wants to go along for a listen, give me a call." Stuffing his notes into a soft-sided briefcase, Nathan adjourned the meeting.

While he tidied up the empty room, Sheridan took an eraser to the whiteboard. "Out of here before ten thirty. I'm proud of you, Nathan."

"Having a productive committee helps." He stuffed a soiled napkin into a stack of empty paper cups and dropped them into a trashcan. "No way I'd hurt Karen's feelings, but I'm a little nervous about this bluegrass band."

"Let's reserve judgment until after we hear them." Sheridan straightened a chair, then rested her hands on the back with an exhausted groan. "Do you suppose Mom had any idea what she was suggesting when she brought up the idea of a fundraiser? I am *so* out of my element!"

"Like I've ever done this before?" Nathan reached for his leather bomber jacket.

"I know, but . . ." Sheridan's shoulders trembled, and Nathan could sense an emotional rockslide getting ready to break loose.

"Hey, don't you dare. Wait till you get home to Kip to go hormonal."

"Oh, stop it. I'm not hormonal, just frustrated." Giving a sniff, Sheridan worked her arms into the sleeves of a cable-knit sweater coat. "The thing is I'm not the organizer Mom is. She could have pulled off this event blindfolded and with both hands—" The words broke off with a tiny choking sound, and Sheridan pressed a fist to her mouth.

Nathan could see in her eyes where her thoughts had taken her, back to that horrible day the Finstons had bound and gagged her and Mom before robbing them. "Sher . . ."

She forced a laugh. "I'm over it, really. It's just . . . everything else piling up. Mom getting married and moving all the way to Texas, you and Kip and I trying to keep things running here, now this fundraiser." Heaving a sigh, she gathered up her purse and notebook. "And the worst of it is I miss teaching way more than I thought I would."

"I didn't realize." Nathan switched off the lights and pulled the classroom door closed behind them.

"I'd hoped working with the clients and volunteers would be a natural transition from my special-ed kids. What I didn't count on was all the planning, paperwork, and people management."

Nathan harrumphed as he held the exit door for his sister. A brisk February breeze nipped at his ears. "Which you never had to do as a teacher? Right, I'm buying that!"

"It was different." Sheridan marched across the nearly empty parking lot and waited for Nathan to unlock the passenger door of his Sonata. "Anyway, remember that spiritual gifts assessment Pastor Alan had the congregation do a few years ago? My gifts were teaching and mercy."

Tossing his briefcase into the backseat, Nathan laughed out loud. "Yeah, I remember how 'merciful' you were to Kip at first. The poor guy's lucky you didn't chase him off the property with a twelve-gauge."

"My point is," Sheridan snapped, yanking her door shut with a bang, "I'm expending too much effort outside my area of giftedness and therefore am feeling grossly unfulfilled."

"Thank you for that explanation, 'Doctor' Lorimer." Nathan started the car. "I suddenly feel grossly in need of a peanut butter fudge milkshake. How about you?"

Sheridan hiked a brow. "Your treat?"

"If it'll keep you from bailing on me before this barbecue cook-off is history."

"I wouldn't, and you know it." Her chest rose and fell on a sigh. "But once we get through this, I really need to rethink my role at Cross Roads Farm, because otherwise I'm liable to burn out completely."

"Fair enough." At the road, Nathan turned in the direction of the Cook Out Restaurant on the other side of Kingsley.

Fifteen minutes later, as they sat in a booth sipping frosty shakes, Nathan allowed his brain to track back through the evening's planning session. Sheridan was definitely right about the advantages of working within one's area of giftedness. Though returning home to manage Cross Roads Farm hadn't fallen within Nathan's original career plans, he found himself thriving in this position of leadership and administration. The fact that he continued his father's legacy only multiplied his sense of satisfaction.

A chunk of peanut butter clogged his straw, and he pulled the straw out to slurp through the other end. Mashing the frozen lump against the roof of his mouth, he eyeballed Sheridan. "That gifts inventory—there wasn't anything on there about music, as I recall."

"Not as a gift of the spirit, no. But music might be one way a gift is expressed, like through worship." Sheridan's cheeks dimpled with another sip of her shake. "What are you getting at?"

"Just thinking about Fil . . . and what you said earlier about burnout. Everybody's always talked about music being Fil's 'gift.' You think she burned out of music because she wasn't using her real gifts?"

"Maybe that's something you should talk to her about." Sheridan's smile brightened into a conspiratorial grin. She flicked her crumpled straw wrapper at him. "Like maybe when you invite *her* to Darlene's Country Diner with you this weekend."

"Darlene's Country Diner? Not familiar with it." Filipa measured a serving of grain into Sundown's feed bucket. The morning had dawned sunny and unusually warm for February, making her glad she'd dressed in layers—and it was time to peel off the flannel shirt.

"Me neither." Nathan caught the shirt she threw at him before she moved on to the next stall. "That's why I thought we could go together. You know the old saying, 'two guinea pigs are better than one?'"

She couldn't hold back a laugh. "Wow, how can I argue with such impeccable logic?"

"So you'll go with me?"

She should just give up and say yes, because clearly Nathan wouldn't stop hounding her until she did. He'd honored his promise to simply be her friend, so this wasn't exactly a date he was asking her on. Anyway, what could happen at a diner?

"All right, I'll think about it." Finishing up with the feed buckets, she snatched her flannel shirt out of Nathan's hands and tied the sleeves around her hips. "But first you have tell me how you heard about this place *and* why you're so gung-ho to try it."

"You think everyone's got an ulterior motive?" Groaning, Nathan jammed his hands into his jeans pockets. When she skewered him with a don't-mess-with-me stare, his mouth flattened. "Okay, I heard about it from Karen Cardenas at the planning meeting last night. Her cousin's in a bluegrass band that's playing there. I need to check them out."

"For the barbecue cook-off?" Filipa huffed and marched past him out the barn door, where she squinted against a blazing blue sky. "And you couldn't just say so. You have to play these mind games with me."

Nathan caught up with her at the gate to the covered arena. "I didn't want you to feel like I was pressuring you to help with the entertainment." His hand clamped down on hers upon the gate latch, and she froze. "But I still would really, really like it if you'd go with me—as a friend. When the band starts up, you can go hang out in the ladies' room if you want. I'll be"—he sniveled—"okay . . . all alone at my table . . . not that you should feel bad for me or anything."

In spite of herself, Filipa burst out laughing. "Nathan, Nathan, Nathan, what am I going to do with you?"

"Wow, you *are* dense if you haven't figured that out yet. You're going to dinner at Darlene's with me." He hooked an elbow around her neck and gave her a noogie on the top of her head.

"Ow!" Breaking free, Filipa charged through the arena gate and yanked it closed between them. "So that's how you treat your friends, is it? Remind me to wear a helmet next time I see you."

Their laughter mingling, Nathan caught her wrists before she could back away from the gate. "Man, it's good to see you smile."

Something tripped inside her. The playfulness in his eyes had warmed into yearning, the same expression he'd worn the day he'd almost kissed her . . . and again the day he did. The bite of rough, cold iron against her palms returned her to reality. "I should get back to work."

Nathan released her arms. "So we're on for Saturday night, right?" He flashed her a double thumbs-up sign as he walked backward toward the cottage.

She waved. "Saturday night." The look of longing had vanished from his eyes, but not without having its effect on her heart.

While she set up some equipment for the afternoon therapy class sessions, Filipa tried yet again to analyze her feelings—about Nathan, about her music, about her life. Yes, she was happy here, happier than she'd been in a very long time. But after almost two months of working at the farm, she'd grown more certain than ever that this was just one stepping stone on the journey toward . . . wherever she was headed.

If she only knew!

Following the diagram the class instructor had given her, she positioned an orange traffic cone, paced off ten steps, then set down the next cone. Everything would be so much easier if God could be equally clear with His directions.

When all the cones were placed, Filipa dragged out several lengths of four-inch PVC pipes to continue shaping the obstacle course. She'd just laid the last grouping when Sheridan strode into the arena.

"Wow, this looks like it'll be fun." Hands on hips, Sheridan examined the layout. "Kassie's getting really creative with her trail courses."

Filipa eased her stiff back. "Wish I could stick around to watch."

Sheridan edged closer, one side of her face hiked in a hopeful grimace. "Any chance you could? Stick around, I mean?"

"Why? Did you need something?" Filipa held her breath. *Please, not more about the fundraiser!*

"Actually, I could really use your help this afternoon. I totally messed up the volunteer schedule, and I'm short three people."

"Oh, no! How'd you manage that?"

"I didn't notice the last student on the class list had dropped off my computer screen, so I didn't schedule volunteers for her." Sheridan pounded her forehead with an open palm. "I tried to tell Nathan last night I do *not* have our mother's gift for organization."

Filipa checked her watch while mentally reviewing her day. No appointments for Papa this afternoon, and the school bus would drop off Naomi, Elisa, and Joseph around four. Filipa could dash home for lunch now, see to

Papa's needs, and leave instructions for Naomi to get supper started.

Deciding the plan would work, Filipa shivered as a tiny thrill spiraled through her chest. All the years her father had worked for the Crosses, all the years she'd been best friends with Nathan, she'd never done more than observe the therapy classes from the sidelines. Either she'd been too young to volunteer or, as years passed, too busy with schoolwork and music studies. Perhaps today she could finally experience firsthand the satisfying blend of fulfillment and pride so often expressed by Nathan and his family.

"Okay," she said with a nervous grin, "tell me what to do."

For the next half hour Sheridan gave her a crash course in a sidewalker's duties—greeting the client upon arrival, adjusting a riding helmet for proper fit, maintaining the correct arm placement for supporting the rider while walking alongside, and sensing how much verbal feedback and redirection to give.

"I had no idea there was so much involved!" Head spinning, Filipa walked with Sheridan out to the pasture to return Gigi, the horse they'd used for demonstrations.

"You'll do fine. I'll put you with an experienced horse leader and sidewalker, so all you have to do is follow their lead."

Apprehensive but excited, Filipa headed home for lunch. When she returned a few hours later, the farm was buzzing with activity. While Kip and Grace tacked horses in the barn, Sheridan parceled out volunteer assignments. Two or three client families had already arrived, and Kassie Kvello, the tall, flame-haired instructor, raved to the parents about how well their children were doing.

"Fil, come on over." Sheridan waved from her spot on the bleachers. "This is Penny Collins. She's going to be your other sidewalker."

"Hi, Penny." Filipa offered her hand to the attractive middle-aged woman standing across from Sheridan. "This is my first time, so tell me if I do anything wrong."

Penny beamed an encouraging smile. "If you love kids and horses, it'll be a snap."

Anticipation sparked as Filipa wondered if this opportunity was God's doing, a chance to explore new directions toward a meaningful career. She did love horses, and she certainly loved her little brothers and sisters.

Well, if she didn't count Charlie's determination to drive her crazy every chance he got, or Naomi's constant chatter about the cutest boys in her class.

Sheridan glanced up from her volunteer chart. "Oh, and here comes your horse leader now." She winked at Filipa. "I think you two have already met."

When Filipa saw Nathan leading Gem into the arena, her stomach bottomed out with a whole different kind of anticipation.

Chapter Ten

"Okay, riders, reverse direction!" Kassie called from the center of the arena.

Keeping the lead rope loose, Nathan gave Janie, his ten-year-old rider, a few seconds to register the instruction and use her reins. A glance over his shoulder brought Filipa into view on Janie's right side. One arm braced against the child's thigh, she looked intent on her sidewalking responsibilities.

And more gorgeous than ever.

Except he had to stop thinking like that. Friendship—that's all Fil was ready for, at least for the time being.

Gem's snort and a trail of green slime up Nathan's sleeve gave him extra incentive to get his thoughts back on track. Even so, he couldn't resist snatching a quick peek at Filipa every chance he got. Her long ponytail poked out through the back of a ball cap, with shiny black wisps escaping at her temples. Every once in a while the breeze would catch a strand, and she'd brush it aside with a finger flick, never once losing her focus on the rider.

And she was catching on fast. When Janie needed to

make Gem turn to the right, Filipa had learned to remind her with a gentle tap on her right hand. If Janie remembered on her own, Filipa showed her delight with an ear-to-ear grin and a sparkle in her eyes that stabbed Nathan straight through the heart.

When the class ended, Filipa hugged her rider and thanked the little girl for "teaching" her so much about being a sidewalker.

Penny Collins opened the arena gate for Nathan to lead Gem out. "She's a natural with kids," Penny said with a nod in Filipa's direction.

"Yeah, I noticed."

"She's Manuelo's daughter, right? The musical prodigy he's always bragging on?"

"That's her." With a tense half-smile, Nathan paused outside the gate and loosened Gem's girth.

Penny smirked as she stepped aside for another volunteer to lead a horse through. "Must be nice to be so multitalented."

"You'd think." Unfortunately, Filipa didn't seem to agree.

Nathan continued to the barn to change Gem's tack. The riders in the next class were much more independent and didn't need sidewalkers, so he figured Sheridan would release Filipa for the day. Too bad, because he'd really been enjoying her nearness.

Good thing he had Saturday night at Darlene's Country Diner to look forward to.

"Nathan, is that you?" Grace's voice drifted over from a neighboring stall. At least he thought it was Grace. She didn't quite sound like herself.

He clipped Gem to the stall tie. "What's up, kiddo?"

"Can you find Kip?"

"He's out at the front pasture getting a horse." After latching Gem's stall door, Nathan paced down the aisle until he glimpsed Grace inside Lady's stall. The horse fidgeted beneath a Southwestern-print saddle pad. The saddle still hung over a rail outside the stall.

Moaning, Grace leaned against the wall and hugged her abdomen. "I'm starting to feel sick. I don't think I can do the next class."

Nathan yanked open the stall door. Looping his arm around her, he led her out to a hay bale. "Just sit here until Kip gets back. We'll find someone to cover for you."

Beads of perspiration dotted the girl's forehead. She rocked forward, clearly in pain. Nathan felt torn between staying close to comfort her and rushing out to yell for Kip to get a move on.

Just then Kip strolled into the barn with Radar. "Hey, you two, no time for—"

"She's sick, Kip." Nathan took Radar's lead rope. "You take care of your sister, I'll take care of the horses."

"Oh, Kip, it hurts so bad!" Completely doubled over now, Grace lifted her chin in a pitiful cry.

Radar nickered, and Nathan glanced behind him to see one of the other horse leaders leading in Gigi for a tack change. "Lee, you're a nurse, aren't you?"

"That's right." The young blonde shifted her glance to where Kip knelt beside Grace. She thrust Gigi's lead rope at Nathan and rushed over. "Where does it hurt, honey?"

Left with both Radar and Gigi, Nathan decided he'd better get them into stalls and out of the way. If the next class started a little late, so be it. He emerged from the second stall to hear Lee saying something about appendicitis and instructing Kip to bring his pickup around. Kip shot Nathan a helpless look as he raced out of the barn.

"Appendicitis? Are you sure?" Nathan marched over to Lee, who rubbed Grace's back with firm but comforting strokes.

"She's got all the signs. I told Kip he should take her straight to the ER. Someone should go with them, though. Kip doesn't need to be distracted while he's driving."

"Right." Thinking fast, Nathan loped across to the arena, barely avoiding being run down by Kip's rusty white pickup. He found Sheridan standing amid a clump of volunteers, her mouth agape.

"What's going on?" she cried, grabbing Nathan's sleeve.

He gave a rapid-fire explanation about Grace. "You should go with them to the hospital. I'll handle things here."

Sheridan didn't waste time with more questions. "I'll get my purse. Don't let them leave without me."

Within minutes the pickup tore down the lane, Kip at the wheel and Sheridan cradling Grace's head against her shoulder. Nathan watched the tailgate disappear in a cloud of dust and sent up a prayer for Grace's health . . . and Kip's driving.

He felt someone's hand creep shyly into his and looked down into Filipa's huge brown eyes. "What can I do to help?" she asked.

Only then did he become aware of the crowd behind him—volunteers, clients, parents, all waiting to be told what happened next.

Guess it was up to him.

Though Filipa had been asked to work only the one class, there was no way she could leave now. With Kip, Sheridan, and Grace on the way to the hospital, Nathan would have his hands full.

He squeezed Filipa's fingers before turning toward the others. "Everything's under control, folks. We just need to do a little regrouping before we get the class started." He asked the parents to have a seat with their kids for a few minutes. Then to Filipa he said, "Grab Sheridan's volunteer schedule."

She jogged over to the bleachers and snatched up the clipboard. Giving the chart a quick glance, she wondered how anyone could make sense of such a jumble. Boxes, circles, arrows, lines. Names crossed out, other names penciled in . . .

Taking the clipboard from her, Nathan scanned the sheet with narrowed eyes, one corner of his mouth twitching into a studious frown. After a few deft strokes with a pencil, he called the volunteers around him. "Lee, Peggy, and Bryan, head over to the barn and tack horses. The list is on the tack room door. I'll be over to help in a minute. Penny, you're Kassie's helper for this class. Fil, make sure the clients each get the right size helmet. Any questions?"

Kassie stepped up beside Nathan. "You've covered everything, but before we get started, let's take a moment to pray for Grace."

The group moved to within hand-holding distance as Kassie spoke a quick prayer, and then everyone hurried off to get ready for the class.

As Filipa fitted helmets on each of the riders, she couldn't stop thinking about how smoothly and efficiently Nathan had taken charge. It wasn't as though she'd never seen this side of him before—he'd been elected class president all four years of high school—but today had brought an even deeper appreciation for his leadership qualities. He was good at what he did, and he did it with natural grace and not a trace of conceit.

A nagging discontent gnawed at her for the rest of the class, a feeling she couldn't quite identify but that seemed to be telling her something important. When the last of the clients and volunteers had left and the horses were returned to their stalls for the night, Nathan found her in the arena as she stacked orange cones to move them off to the side.

Nathan wrested the heavy cones out of her arms. "You've been at this practically all day. You must be exhausted."

"Just glad I could stick around to help." She adjusted her cap before bending to grab one end of a PVC pipe. "Have you heard anything more about Grace?"

"Got a call from Kip a few minutes ago. They're prepping her for an emergency appendectomy." Nathan set the cones next to the rail and then scooped up an armful of PVC pipes. "I never heard Kip so scared. He's usually the calm one."

Ignoring the ache across her shoulders, Filipa added another pipe to the pile Nathan had started near the cones. "Maybe you should go be with them at the hospital. I'll finish up here."

He chewed his lip, hesitation darkening his eyes. "Somebody's got to do the evening chores."

"Let me." She rested a hand on his arm. "Go be with your family. I can see how worried you are."

With a sigh, Nathan palmed the back of Filipa's neck and pulled her close to rest his chin on top of her head.

"Thanks for understanding. Truth is I've started thinking of Grace like my own little sister."

"Then get going. Now." She shoved him toward the arena gate. "I promise, things'll be fine here."

Or so she hoped. As she watched Nathan drive away, an eerie quiet descended upon the farm, along with lengthening shadows and a growing chill in the air as clouds moved in to obscure the setting sun. Then, as she went in search of the jacket she'd left lying somewhere, she realized Nathan hadn't explained exactly what "evening chores" entailed.

Papa could fill her in, though. Finding her jacket draped over a saddle rack in the tack room, she slid her arms into the sleeves and tugged her cell phone from the pocket. She plopped onto a hay bale to make the call. When Elisa answered, Filipa had her put Papa on the line.

"I need to be here awhile longer, Papa. Grace got sick. They had to take her to the hospital." She explained about the emergency surgery.

"*Pobrecita*—poor child! So you are there all alone?"

"I promised Nathan I'd take care of things." Filipa wrinkled her nose. "Except I'm not sure what needs to be done."

Her father gave a low chuckle. "Evening chores are not hard. Check that all the horses are secure in their stalls, refill the water pails, and make sure each horse has a fresh flake of hay."

A steady patter drew Filipa's attention toward the roof, just as a gust of wind blew moisture through the open barn door. "Oh, great. It's raining."

Papa's voice took on the faintest hint of concern. "I do not hear thunder. Perhaps it is only a passing shower."

Filipa crossed the barn and stepped inside the tack

room, removing her father's yellow slicker from its hook behind the door. "Don't worry, Papa. If this turns into a storm, I know better than to go anywhere near Jet."

"See that you don't. But go now and turn on the radio in Jet's barn. Music sometimes distracts him while masking the sounds from outside."

"Good idea." Disconnecting, she jogged straight to the small barn and found a portable radio hanging from a rafter near Jet's stall. When she pressed the power button, gentle music from a classical radio station filled the barn—the haunting strains of *Valse Triste*, by Sibelius. A wave of nostalgia swept through her, muscle memory bringing subtle tremors to fingers that had played this piece for her senior year piano recital.

The rustle of shavings drew her attention to Jet's stall. The big black horse lifted his head over the gate and craned his neck toward her with a curious nicker. She couldn't resist stepping close enough to rub his velvet muzzle. In the next stall, Ember peeked out and whinnied as if demanding his share of the attention.

"All right, all right." Filipa laughed and went to scratch the friendly horse behind the ears. "Now I've really got to get back to my chores. You two behave—"

A clap of thunder shook the rafters as the drizzling rain became a downpour. Jet neighed and kicked at his stall door, then began pacing, his head held high and his eyes flicking nervously. Filipa's stomach clenched. If Jet's anxiety rose any higher, she feared for what he might do—to himself, or to her if she couldn't keep him contained.

Realizing the rain hammering the roof was beginning to drown out the radio, she dashed across the aisle to turn up the volume. Another familiar piece now poured forth from the speakers, and Filipa's trained ear recognized immediately the stylings of Australian classical guitarist John Williams. She'd never heard a more beautiful rendition of Tárrega's *Recuerdos de la Alhambra.*

Tears sprang to her eyes, and she rushed from the barn, stopping only when she reached the open doorway at the far end of the main barn. Gazing toward the darkened arena through a curtain of rain, she sucked in massive gulps of damp air and prayed for the storm to pass.

"Your sister's out of surgery, Mr. Lorimer. It was completely routine."

Nathan turned from the window to see Kip rise and draw Sheridan into a hug. They thanked the nurse for the good news. "When can we see her?" Kip asked.

"As soon as she's out of recovery. Why don't you get something to eat and come back in an hour or so?"

The nurse left, and Nathan joined Kip and Sheridan as they collected their things. "I should get back to the farm," Nathan said. "I left Fil there by herself, and she's not answering her cell." He shot an uneasy glance toward the window.

Kip followed his gaze. "Rain? Been so preoccupied I didn't even notice."

"The clouds look even heavier out our way." Nathan shrugged into his bomber jacket.

Reaching up to straighten Nathan's collar, Sheridan beamed an encouraging smile. "Filipa's too smart to take any risks. If Jet busts out of his stall again, she'll have the good sense to get out of the way."

"Hope you're right." Nathan walked with his sister and brother-in-law to the elevator. When Sheridan and Kip got off at the cafeteria floor, he told them to give Grace his love before continuing down to the parking level.

At least it hadn't rained hard enough or long enough to flood the low-water crossing. By the time Nathan reached the blue-and-yellow Cross Roads Farm sign, the rain had lessened to little more than a heavy mist. His headlights swept Manuelo's old blue pickup where Filipa had parked it next to the cottage, and he eased the Sonata in beside it.

The mercury vapor pole light cast the lane in an eerie pink glow as Nathan sidestepped puddles on his way to the barn. "Fil? You out here?"

No reply. The only sound was the rustle of shavings as horses stirred in their stalls. Then Nathan's ears picked up radio music drifting from the small barn beyond. He looked into a couple of stalls on his way through, noting the water pails were full and the horses had been fed. In the small barn he found both Jet and Ember contentedly munching on hay. Since the storm had ceased, he flicked off the radio and then offered Jet and Ember each a peppermint. "So what did y'all do with Fil, huh? Hope you didn't scare her so bad she ran screaming into the night."

"Not hardly."

He spun around at the sound of her voice. "Hey! I was starting to get worried." Well, there was no *starting to* about it. He'd hardly been able to get her off his mind since the first raindrops hit the waiting-room window. "I tried to call. Is your cell turned off?"

"Guess I didn't hear it—or maybe the battery's dead. I was just up at the house feeding the dogs. Figured they must be getting hungry by now." Dark circles beneath Filipa's eyes gave her a haunted look. "How's Grace?"

"She's in recovery. Everything went fine." He stepped

toward Filipa and ran a finger beneath a stray lock of her silky black hair. "You look beat, Fil."

Her jaw flexed. She lowered her gaze. "Long day."

Except . . . this looked like more than simple fatigue after a hard day's work. The light he'd seen in her eyes these last few weeks—even more evident while she'd been helping as a sidewalker this afternoon—had vanished. He wanted to ask what had changed, but she didn't appear willing to talk.

He draped an arm around her shoulders. "I'm starved. Thought I'd whip up an omelet. Wanna join me?"

"Guess so." He felt her weariness as she leaned into him.

In the cottage he helped her out of her jacket and then made her stretch out on the sofa while he cracked eggs into a bowl, gave them a whisk, then slid them in a buttered skillet. "Okay if I add some bell pepper and grated cheese?"

"Sure."

Filipa's monosyllabic replies heightened Nathan's sense that something was wrong. He reined in the urge to pressure her into talking and instead concentrated on letting the omelet set up just right before folding it onto a plate. He moved half to a second plate, collected a couple of forks and napkins, and then carried everything to the coffee table.

Filipa sighed and sat up. "Smells good. I'm hungrier than I realized."

Relieved to see a little color return to her cheeks, Nathan settled in next to her. They ate without speaking, the only sound the scrape of flatware against Aztec-patterned plates.

When they finished, Nathan rose and carried their dishes to the sink. He opened the fridge. "Want a soda? Or how about some milk or juice?"

"Just a glass of water. Then I should get home." Filipa

joined him in the narrow kitchen, and her nearness as she edged behind him to pull a glass from the cupboard made his stomach do weird things with the omelet he'd just downed.

After pouring a glass of milk for himself, Nathan leaned against the fridge. He couldn't muffle his concern any longer. "Fil . . . you okay?"

Her mouth formed a smile, but a kind of grief shone in her eyes, as if she'd lost something very dear. She sipped her water, then set down the glass. "Thanks for the omelet. You're a good cook, Nathan." Her glance drifted sideways for a moment. "And you were amazing this afternoon. The way you took charge of the volunteers—it was like you were in your element."

"Thanks." He massaged the back of his neck, feeling warmth rising. Though he appreciated her praise, he sensed there was more behind her words than just a compliment to his administrative skills.

Filipa strode to the chair where Nathan had laid her jacket. "Now I've really got to go. If I don't head straight to bed, I'll never make it back by six in the morning."

"Sleep in, why don't you? You've earned it." Nathan followed her to the door, his whole body aching to hold her, comfort her, chase away whatever demons had robbed her of the peace she craved.

"I'll be fine after a good night's sleep." She poked around in a pocket until she pulled out a set of keys. One hand on the door jamb, she paused and glanced back at Nathan. "But, um, I think I'd better cancel on those dinner plans for Saturday."

Her words hit Nathan like a sucker punch to the gut. "Are you sure?"

"I could really use a lazy Saturday evening at home. You

know, wash my hair, do my nails." As if to convince him, she extended her hands to display broken fingernails and ragged cuticles.

The sight of those hands cracked Nathan's heart like the eggs he'd just broken to make their omelet. If he didn't think she'd wrench them away, he'd take her hands and cradle them against his chest.

And kiss her again until her senses returned and she realized how she'd been throwing her life away these past few months.

Lord, show me how to help her. And maybe, while You're at it, let her know how badly I want to be more than just "best friends."

Chapter Eleven

Seated on a scratchy sofa in the cardiac rehab waiting area, Filipa browsed through a year-old *People* magazine while waiting for her father. She glanced up occasionally to watch his progress. Still in physical therapy for his knee, he couldn't work up much of a sweat on a treadmill or stationary bike, but he could pedal like crazy with his arms. No doubt about it, Papa was strong and determined.

Determined to reclaim his job at the farm and send Filipa back to music school, if he had his way. He caught her eye and shot her a look-at-me grin while pedaling even faster.

Show-off. Filipa rolled her eyes and returned her attention to the magazine page, feigning extreme fascination with whatever Prince Harry had been in the news about last year.

A vibration rumbled from the pocket of her purse, tucked between her hip and the armrest. She tugged out her cell phone and recognized the same New York number she'd been ignoring for the past six months. Couldn't the guy take a hint?

Maybe it was time to answer the call and tell it to him straight. Tossing aside the magazine, she marched outside to the atrium. "Hello?"

"Miss Beltran! Don't you ever check your messages? And *please* don't tell me you're still in South Carolina?"

"*North* Carolina. And yes, I am." She muted a sigh. "How are you, Mr. Benjamin?"

Her former music performance professor huffed. "Quite unhappy you haven't returned to school yet, Miss Beltran. I fully expected this *break* of yours to end when classes resumed after the Christmas holidays."

"Then you misread my intentions." She toed a brown leaf that had fallen from a ficus tree. "I don't plan to return at all."

"You can't mean that!" Indignation laced Mr. Benjamin's tone. "You can't deprive the world of your talent. That would be the ultimate crime."

Filipa glanced up as the outer door opened and a young mother pushed her severely handicapped child through in a wheelchair. The sight triggered images of yesterday's equine therapy classes. Children with autism, Down syndrome, cerebral palsy, emotional or behavioral problems, and countless other special needs—the staff and volunteers at Cross Roads Farm were making a difference in these kids' lives.

Suddenly everything she'd been trying to puzzle out for the last six months began to crystallize. It wasn't the music she'd come to despise but the total self-absorption, the blind obsession with mastering the next level of proficiency. How many times had she labored for hours to learn a single complicated transition? How many times had she practiced the same musical phrase again and again and again because it wasn't "perfect"? She'd studied and rehearsed and auditioned and performed until not a shred of joy remained.

And what purpose did it all serve? Could a flawlessly played cadenza heal a broken child, end famine, usher in world peace?

Through the phone she heard the reedy tones of an oboe, then Mr. Benjamin's muffled criticism, "No, no, no! Do you not comprehend *accelerando*? This isn't a funeral dirge!"

"Mr. Benjamin," Filipa began, empathy surging for the browbeaten oboist.

"Yes, sorry. Just tell me when I can expect you back. This extended break of yours has gone on long enough."

She sensed nothing she could say would matter. "It's more than a break, sir. It's a complete change of direction." *Which* direction, she had yet to determine, but knowing that much was a huge start. "So please don't look for my return. Goodbye, Mr. Benjamin."

Tucking the phone into her purse, she gradually became aware of music being piped in through overhead speakers. Recognizing the Barry Manilow oldie, she hummed along as she entered the cardiac rehab waiting area to check on her father.

Then it suddenly dawned on her that the music must always have been playing every time she'd brought Papa here. There'd been music at the physical therapy center as well. And how many times had she found the radio playing in the barn when she'd arrived for work each morning? Had she become so adept at closing her mind and her ears that she no longer even heard the music?

She froze. *Dear Lord, have I been tuning You out, too?*

Saturday mornings were always extra busy at Cross Roads Farm, and today Filipa had made a point of arriving even earlier than usual. She wanted to finish the barn chores well before the therapy classes began in case Sheridan might find a spot for her in the volunteer schedule.

After trundling the last load of manure to the collection bin, she caught up with Kip on his way into the barn. "How's Grace doing?"

"Chompin' at the bit to get back on a horse again." Kip glanced into a freshly cleaned stall, then slanted Filipa a look beneath the brim of his Stetson. "You're done already? What time did you get here, anyway?"

"Oh, I don't know . . . five-ish?" She followed him into the tack room. "Is it too early to get the first group of horses ready?"

"You can help me with tack." Kip consulted a list and then handed her an English saddle and fuzzy pad. "This is for Belle."

Filipa took the saddle and pad and draped them over the rack outside Belle's stall. Returning to the tack room, she waited for Kip's next instructions. As he stretched to reach a bridle on an upper hook, his leg brushed aside a white sheet, revealing the pommel and skirt of the most beautiful Western saddle Filipa had ever seen.

Breathing out an awed sigh, she stepped closer to brush her fingers across the hand-tooled leather. "Is this new? It's gorgeous!"

Kip grinned as he drew back the sheet. "I'm makin' it for the barbecue cook-off. This'll be the grand prize."

"You *made* it?" Filipa jerked back her arm as if she might somehow mar this work of art with her work-soiled hands. "I heard you used to have a saddle-making business, but I had no idea . . ." Again, she dared to touch the intricate design. "This is amazing! It must have taken you hours."

If a cowboy could blush, Kip just did. He tipped his Stetson toward the back of his head and appeared to admire his own handiwork. "Sher calls it my 'labor of love.' I just call it doin' what makes me happy. And if it brings someone else joy, I'm even happier."

Another piece of Filipa's puzzle fell into place.

Four hours later, when she finally had time to catch her breath, she sank onto the top tier of the bleachers. The arena stood empty now, but the smells of dirt and horse sweat still lingered. In the pasture beyond, she glimpsed Belle and Gigi enjoying a roll in the dust and yanking up tufts of winter rye. Even the horses seemed happy just being themselves. And after filling in again this morning for absent volunteers, Filipa suspected more than a few of those horses took particular pleasure in being exactly the mount their special rider needed.

"Still here?" Nathan strode toward her, a lopsided grin curling his lips.

She clasped her hands around one knee. "Just savoring the quiet before I head home for lunch. When all the kids are home from school for the weekend, it gets a little crazy over there."

"You really pitched in again today." Nathan climbed the bleachers to sit beside her. "Kip said you were here way early."

Filipa covered a yawn. "Yeah, I could really use a nap." She slid her gaze his way with a smirk. "Especially if I'm going to be out late tonight listening to this bluegrass band some guy wants me to hear."

Nathan studied his reflection in the bathroom mirror, then wet his comb and launched another attack on the tuft of hair that refused to lie flat after his shower. He'd been as antsy as a flea on a scratching dog ever since Fil dropped her bombshell on him earlier.

What changed her mind—again?

Well, he sure wasn't about to look a gift horse in the mouth. Besides, it wasn't Filipa's teeth he was interested in. It was . . . everything else about her.

Finally satisfied his hair wouldn't break into a Dagwood Bumstead imitation halfway through dinner, he finished buttoning his shirt, tucked it into his jeans, and fastened his belt buckle. Slipping on a brown tweed blazer, he grabbed his wallet and keys and headed out.

When he pulled into the Beltrans' driveway five minutes later, another nervous twinge made his palms sweat. He scraped them up and down his jeans a few times before hauling in a deep breath and marching up to the front door.

Rosa Beltran answered, her stiff smile somewhere between curiosity and protectiveness. "Good evening, Nathan. Won't you come in?"

"Thanks, ma'am." He wiped his boots on the doormat before stepping inside.

Manuelo nodded from his recliner. "You and Filipa will be late?"

Definitely a hint of fatherly suspicion in the man's tone. Nathan wondered if Filipa's parents knew something he didn't. Like, had Filipa suggested this might be an actual *date*? Good grief, how many times over the years had Nathan and Fil gone out together—*as friends*—and her parents never so much as blinked?

He was about to reply with a promise to have Fil home

by eleven when she strode in from the hallway. One look at her in those curve-hugging indigo jeans and a deep purple V-neck sweater that made her dark eyes look even bigger and more luminous than ever, and he imagined the look on his face was giving Fil's parents plenty of reason to worry.

"Close your mouth, Nathan. You'll catch flies." Filipa tossed her hair off her shoulder. "Don't you dare say I 'clean up nicely,' or I'll have Charlie take you out back and give you what-for."

Her brother's voice carried from somewhere in the kitchen. "Hey, don't drag me into this. Marry her, dude, and get her out of here so she'll quit nagging me to give back her old room."

Nathan's lungs spasmed in a single choking cough. "Uh, maybe we should go?"

"Let's." Filipa grabbed a jacket from the front closet. "Good night, Mama. Good night, Papa. Don't wait up, okay?" A millisecond later she was out the door, and Nathan didn't waste any time catching up.

As he started the car, she glanced at him with a crooked smile. "Believe me, I have no idea what that was all about."

Still speechless, Nathan could only raise a brow and shrug. They rode in tense silence for the better part of five miles, Charlie's remark frosting the atmosphere between them like a late-winter ice storm.

Maybe the best thing to do was acknowledge the awkwardness and laugh it off. "So," Nathan began, "Charlie must want you out of the house pretty badly if he's willing to marry you off to a hick like me." He faked a belch and pretended to pick his nose.

"Yuck!" Filipa averted her face and pressed into the door panel. "If you do that at dinner, I'm out of there!"

They both laughed, and Nathan began to relax. "I guess

you must be feeling the pinch of being in close quarters with your family again after so long away."

"No kidding, especially those first several weeks sleeping on the sofa. But once my parents accepted I'd be around for a while, they let me move in with Naomi and Elisa. It's crowded but at least it's a real bed."

After merging onto the highway, Nathan slid her a quick glance. "Any further thoughts on how long 'a while' is going to be?"

"I'm still figuring things out." Did he detect a shade more confidence in her voice? "For the time being, I'm happy helping at home and filling in for Papa at the farm." She definitely did sound happy again. "And subbing for volunteers this past week was more fun and rewarding than I expected. Cross Roads Farm is doing something really special for those kids."

"We are, aren't we?" Nathan couldn't stop a proud smile from turning up the corners of his mouth. He reached across the space between them to clasp Filipa's hand. "Glad you're a part of it."

Her gaze met his, and she returned his smile. "Me, too."

Yes, there'd definitely been some changes in Filipa over the past few days, and Nathan liked what he saw. He liked it a lot.

When Nathan returned his grip to the steering wheel, Filipa's hand felt suddenly cold. Charlie's stupid comment about marriage couldn't have been more off-base, but tonight Filipa found herself mentally exploring possibilities she hadn't allowed herself to even acknowledge before now.

Nathan as more than a friend? He'd certainly implied

he could be interested in more. As if that single passionate kiss in the Crosses' kitchen weren't enough, how could she deny his tender glances or the tingles that shot up her spine at his slightest touch?

Dear Lord, is it time to give this a chance?

They arrived at the diner in Pineville to find the parking lot overflowing into the street out front and the alley in back. "Good thing I made reservations," Nathan said as he pulled into a parking space farther up the street.

As they started along the sidewalk, Nathan eased his arm around her back. The protective gesture warmed her, while the feel of Nathan's hip brushing hers quickened her pulse. She looked toward the diner, where at least thirty people mingled on the neon-lit cabin-style front porch, many of them holding pagers with blinking LEDs. "Do you suppose all these people are here for the band?"

"Karen did say they were pretty good." Nathan shouldered through the crowd until they reached the front door. Inside the lobby he gave his name to the hostess.

She grabbed menus and two packets of silverware rolled into blue bandana-print napkins. "Right this way, Mr. Cross."

When they arrived at a table for two just left of center stage, Filipa tugged at Nathan's sleeve. "Wow, how much did you bribe her?"

"Not a cent." Pulling out Filipa's chair, Nathan leaned close to her ear. "Although when I called in the reservation, I may have insinuated we were talent scouts."

"Nathan, you didn't!"

"Isn't that why we're here?" He scooted his chair in across from her.

"Yes, but—" Filipa shook her head. One look at his boyish grin and he could have sold her on pretending they were visiting royalty from Greater Berserkistan. She screened a fit of giggles behind her menu. Life with Nathan was certainly anything but dull!

They tossed any diet or health concerns aside and splurged on chicken-fried steak with mashed potatoes and cream gravy, buttery squash casserole, fried okra, and peach cobbler. Filipa could barely finish half her meal, and even after Nathan stole several bites from her plate, she still had plenty to fill a takeout container.

While they waited for the band to take the stage, Filipa excused herself to visit the ladies' room. She returned to find Nathan had moved their chairs together behind the table.

He rose slightly as she took her seat. "I ordered us a couple of decafs. Hope that's okay."

The rich aroma of brewed coffee wafted from heavy stoneware mugs. Filipa stirred in a dollop of cream and then sipped appreciatively. "Exactly what I needed to top off this decadent meal."

"So you're glad you came?"

She shot him a raised-eyebrow stare. "I'll let you know after we hear the band."

Moments later a petite blonde dressed in jeans and a rhinestone-studded denim jacket stepped to center stage. "Welcome to Darlene's Country Diner, folks. Please give a big hand to tonight's guest performers, the Piedmont Valley Drifters."

Six men with longish hair and neatly trimmed beards strolled onstage, their attire an eclectic mix of scruffy jeans, black T-shirts, and fringed leather jackets. One settled in behind a drum set, while another stood at an electric keyboard. The other four included the lead guitarist, fiddler, mandolinist, and electric bass player.

From the moment they struck their first chord, Filipa found herself captivated. She'd never been much of a bluegrass fan, and this band was far from polished. But their enthusiasm bubbled over, infusing every song with foot-stomping, get-up-out-of-your-seat fun. When the first set ended, Filipa's palms stung from clapping so hard.

Reaching for her water glass, she became aware that sometime during the performance Nathan had edged his chair even closer to hers. His arm encircled her, his face so near that his cheek brushed hers. With a gasp she turned toward him, and at the same moment he swiveled to look at her. His lips parted. His gaze drifted to her mouth.

Only the fact that they were seated in a busy, bustling restaurant kept Filipa from melting into Nathan's arms and returning the kiss she saw in his eyes. She pressed her fingertips to her own lips and faced forward. "Please, Nathan," she murmured, quick breaths freezing her lungs.

He stiffened, apparently as caught off guard as she. Withdrawing his arm, he rested one elbow on the table and took a swig of coffee that must be ice-cold by now. He grimaced as he swallowed. "So what'd you think of the Piedmont Valley Drifters? Should we see if we can book them for the cook-off, or do we need to hear a few more bands?"

She cleared her throat, gaze locked on her folded hands. "I think it's safe to say you've found what you were looking for."

Chapter Twelve

Nathan had found what he was looking for, all right. Didn't take much convincing to realize he was falling deeper in love every day. And so was Filipa, if his male intuition counted for anything.

Male. Intuition. Could you use those two words together in the same sentence? Oxymoron or not, Nathan was definitely picking up a whole new set of vibes from his longtime best friend. Maybe she wasn't nearly as ready to admit her feelings as he was, but in the weeks since their evening at Darlene's Country Diner, they sure seemed to be growing closer. Besides several "lunch dates" at his cottage after she finished morning barn chores, a couple of Sunday-evening Scrabble tournaments with Kip and Sheridan (okay, so he'd practically had to hogtie Kip to the game table to get him to play), and a long, lazy trail ride one Saturday afternoon, Nathan had finally talked Filipa into coming to the fundraiser planning meetings.

He'd known all along she would have a lot to contribute, but he'd still been amazed at how quickly she became a team player, diving right in to their sometimes heated discussions about budgets, promotion, and setup.

The following Monday night was no exception. When Peggy Abbott reported that she still couldn't convince the event equipment supplier to provide tables and chairs at no cost, Filipa sat back and crossed her arms. "Have you given them a good reason to *want* to?"

Peggy swiveled sideways, her tone defensive. "Besides phoning several times, I've mailed them tons of info about Cross Roads Farm—newsletters, brochures, annual reports. They agree it's a worthy cause, but the best they've offered so far is a twenty-percent discount."

"They agree it's a worthy cause *in principle*," Filipa said with conviction."So is Habitat for Humanity or World Vision or the ASPCA. How many of you get those computer-generated pleas in your mailbox every month and pitch them straight into the recycle bin?"

Murmurs of agreement circled the table. Nathan flicked his pen against his legal pad, a light-bulb moment zapping his brain. "I see what you're getting at, Fil. To this corporation we're just one more charity with its hand out. We have to find a way to get them personally invested in Cross Roads Farm."

"Exactly." Filipa sat forward, hands clasped on the edge of the table. "Just look at the corporate sponsors we've already signed up. They're mainly local businesses we all deal with regularly. They already know what this program is about, and its success matters to them."

Sheridan rose and went to the whiteboard, where Nathan had posted the current list of donors and sponsors. Another column listed several businesses they were still hoping to gain commitments from, including the equipment rental company. Taking a red marker, Sheridan put a checkmark by four names in the "waiting on" column. "Every one of these companies is either a big-city business concern or part of a national chain. Filipa's right. They simply don't have the personal connection with Cross Roads Farm that the local businesses do."

"But since we need the goods or services they offer, how do we change that?" Nathan had a few ideas of his own, but he hoped the other team members would step in with suggestions.

"We could visit with the managers in person," someone suggested.

"What if we took our kids with us? If they could see how much the program has helped my son—"

"How about sending them a DVD montage of our classes—"

"—with testimonials from parents and riders?"

"And volunteers, too. Don't forget us."

Nathan scribbled down ideas as fast as the team members spit them out. He shared a glance with Filipa and could see from the sparkle in her eyes that she'd effectively made her point.

When the flow of suggestions tapered off, Filipa spoke again. "Look, I know I'm the newest member of this group, but my father has worked at Cross Roads Farm since I was a little girl. The truth is, even though I practically grew up at the farm, I pretty much took what they do there for granted. It wasn't until Nathan and Sheridan roped me in as an emergency volunteer substitute a few weeks ago that I really began to appreciate the miracles God is performing through this program."

At the word *miracles*, several team members nodded in agreement. Sheridan reached for Filipa's arm and gave it a grateful squeeze.

"What I'm trying to say," Filipa continued, "is that while all these ideas are good ones, nothing will be more effective than bringing people to Cross Roads Farm to experience for themselves what the program is all about."

Bev Williams cocked her head. "I agree, but how do we convince them to take time out of their busy schedules to visit? We've tried that with Pine Valley Haven without much success."

Filipa looked toward Nathan, the passion in her eyes giving way to doubt.

But Nathan had picked up her enthusiasm, and already his mind was spinning with the possibilities. "In the business world people expect some kind of return on their investment, whether it's time, money, or goods and services. We need to offer these potential supporters something in return—something more immediate than an end-of-the-year tax write-off."

"In other words," Peggy Abbott said, "you have to spend money in order to make money."

Dave Williams tapped his chin. "Where are you going with this, Nathan?"

"What if we hold a mini-fundraiser in advance of the main event?" He ignored the panicked look on Sheridan's face. "Nothing extravagant—more of a friendly show-and-tell. We extend personal invitations to the owners and managers of these businesses, have them out to the farm for a catered meal, and let them observe an actual class session."

"I like it," Karen Cardenas burst out. "And they could hear firsthand from clients and volunteers what the program means to them."

Sheridan massaged her temple as she studied the calendar app on her smartphone. "If we're going to do this in time for the cook-off, we have to schedule it soon."

She cast Nathan a helpless look. "But I can't possibly juggle one more thing *and* keep up with the regular classes."

"No worries, sis. I've got this." Nathan was already mentally working out the logistics. It wouldn't be easy tossing in a sponsorship event on top of all they were already doing. But if this plan garnered the support necessary to make the cook-off a success, then the additional effort would be worth it.

Flipping to a new page in his legal pad, Nathan jotted a few more notes, then told the group he'd email them within the next few days with additional details. In the meantime, he turned their attention to the next order of business.

Forty minutes later Nathan wrapped up the meeting with a quick summary of where they stood. "We have five barbecue teams signed up, including my new stepfather, who's bringing a team all the way from Texas. We have flyers up all around town and in neighboring communities. Sheridan will pick up the printed invitations on Friday, so by next Monday's meeting I'll need addresses for any friends, family members, and acquaintances you'd like included in the mailing."

With that, the meeting adjourned. Filipa had ridden into town with Nathan and Sheridan, so the drive back to the farm gave Nathan a chance to tell Filipa how much he appreciated her ideas. But he held off expressing how he really felt until he dropped off Sheridan and parked in Filipa's driveway.

He reached across the console to tweak a lock of her hair. "Do you have any idea what your support means to me? I couldn't do this without you, Fil."

She quirked her lips. "You were doing fine before you coerced me into coming to your meetings."

Nathan grinned. "Admit it, you kind of enjoyed the fireworks tonight."

Lifting her chin, Filipa locked her arms in a stubborn pose, but she couldn't quite hide a teasing smile. "Can I help it if I'm passionate about Cross Roads Farm? That's entirely *your* fault."

Nathan suddenly didn't want to talk about the fundraiser or the farm or anything else that didn't involve gathering this woman in his arms and showing her how fast he was falling for her. "I love seeing you so *alive* again. I love seeing you care about something this much." His tone mellowed. "Most of all, I love that we're in this together."

Her gaze shifted to meet his, and the shimmer in her eyes made his heart flip-flop. "Are we, Nathan? Together, I mean?"

He cocked his head, looking at her as if that was the stupidest question anyone ever asked. "Don't you get it, Fil? I'm crazy in love with you."

A tiny gasp whispered between her lips, and her eyes widened in surprise. A second later she offered a shy smile. "Then you'll understand why I'm about to tell you good night and go inside."

Now it was Nathan's turn to look surprised. "But I—"

"It's late," she said, reaching for the door handle, "and my boss would be very annoyed if I overslept and didn't make it to work on time in the morning." As she exited the car, her tortured expression seemed to plead for understanding. "Good night, Nathan. I'll see you tomorrow."

He watched in frustration as she marched through the front door without so much as a parting glance. *Dear God, what will it take for her to admit she loves me back?*

Oh, Father, give me the courage to say the words Nathan longs to hear.

Because she did love him, more deeply than she ever imagined possible. But how could she admit how terrified she was of giving in to these feelings? For nearly a decade every ounce of her focus had been bent toward her music—toward mastery, toward perfection.

Toward fulfilling her parents' dreams.

And though Mama and Papa had eased up considerably on pressuring her to return to school, they hadn't completely masked their disappointment. Enduring their tacit disapproval day after day only compounded Filipa's insecurity. She needed direction. She needed purpose. Until she found it, letting herself fall in love would be just one more way of dodging her doubts and questions. She wouldn't do that to Nathan—she loved him too much.

As she closed the door behind her, Mama looked up from sewing on a button. "It was a long meeting?"

"There was a lot to discuss." Filipa hung her sweater in the entryway closet.

"Come and sit for a moment. Tell me about it." Mama nodded toward the end of the sofa nearest her chair.

Filipa collapsed onto the cushions, not at all sure she felt up to rehashing the planning meeting, especially since Nathan now completely preoccupied her thoughts. So she said the first thing that popped into her mind: "Mama, I'm scared."

Her mother's head jerked up. "Of what?"

"Of making another mistake." Exhaustion overwhelming her, Filipa rested her head on the arm of the sofa.

Mama tied off and snipped the thread behind the button she'd been reattaching. Poking her needle into a pincushion, she heaved a sigh. "Mistakes are part of living. The only way to avoid them is to cease even to try."

A sudden sob choked Filipa. "I'm sorry, Mama. I've tried to be the perfect daughter—tried my hardest to live up to your expectations—but I just can't do it anymore."

"Oh, my dear one!" Tossing aside her mending, Mama shoved up from her chair and sank onto the sofa next to Filipa. She cradled her weeping daughter's head against her chest and rocked gently. "Your papa and I have never expected you to be perfect. We have only desired your happiness and fulfillment."

Sniffling, Filipa raised her head. She searched her mother's face. "Can you still love me if I don't return to music school? If I never pick up my guitar again?"

Hurt filled her mother's eyes. "How can you ask such a thing?"

"Because I know how disappointed you are."

"Do you suppose God loves His children any less when they disappoint Him? No, He only desires all the more to draw them into His arms and heal their hurts." Mama pressed Filipa's head against her shoulder once more. "Ah, *mija*, I have also made mistakes—none greater than causing you to doubt my love. Please forgive me."

They sat together in the quiet living room, Filipa resting in her mother's comforting embrace until sleep beckoned. Six a.m. would come soon enough. She straightened and kissed her mother's cheek. "Thank you, Mama. Thank you for being patient with me while I find my way again."

Cradling Filipa's face in her work-worn hands, Mama

offered a sad smile. "God knows the way. In His time, He will show you."

In the bedroom she now shared with her sisters, Filipa undressed in the dark, careful not to wake them. Snuggled beneath a fuzzy blanket in their double bed, the girls looked peaceful. They'd grown so much while Filipa had been away at school. Naomi had blossomed into a smart, capable young teen who aced every science and math test. Elisa, ever quiet and thoughtful, was the family's most prolific reader. Where would their futures take them?

Crawling beneath the covers in her narrow bed by the wall, Filipa said a prayer for her siblings. She prayed they would each find their own path, never doubting either their family's love or God's.

Over the next few days Nathan grew so busy with the latest fundraiser plans that Filipa saw very little of him during her hours at the farm. She missed spending time with him, but at least his busyness gave her breathing space. More than ever, she sensed God was doing a major work in her life, and she wanted to give Him all the room He required.

Feeling the need for a fresh perspective, the following Sunday Filipa decided to visit Nathan's church rather than worship with her family at the Catholic church where she'd grown up. After hurrying through chores at the farm, she took a quick shower and made it in time for the ten-thirty service, finding a seat moments before Nathan arrived with Kip and Sheridan. She wiggled her fingers in a hesitant wave.

Nathan's eyes lit up. He signaled Kip and Sheridan to go on ahead and then slipped into the pew next to Filipa.

Her nerves sang at his closeness—even more when he tucked her hand into his own. He bent toward her ear. "How about a horseback ride this afternoon?"

She nodded. "I'll come over later."

In the meantime, Pastor Wolfe's message gave Filipa even more to think about. He spoke on the many varieties of God's gifts: His peace, His Son, the Holy Spirit, new life in Christ, the various gifts of the Spirit, the skills and abilities necessary for meaningful work.

"'Every good and perfect gift is from above, coming down from the Father of the heavenly lights, who does not change like shifting shadows,'" the pastor read from the book of James. "Friends, as you move into the week ahead, take a look around and see all the good things the Lord has brought into your life—home and family, friendships, talents and skills, hopes and dreams. Are you taking those gifts for granted? Or are you using and appreciating them for all they're worth?"

Filipa pictured her beautiful Paulino Bernabe guitar, untouched for months, tucked away in its case in the back of Naomi and Elisa's closet. After all these years, she still wondered who had provided such a generous gift. Her own parents could never have afforded this extravagant gesture, and she seriously doubted any of her former music teachers had that kind of money to spare. But who else could possibly have taken such a personal interest in her music career?

And what would this person think today knowing she had simply walked away from it all?

Later, when the family had finished lunch and the younger children had gone outside for a backyard game of kickball, Filipa went to the closet and pushed aside clothing and shoes until she unearthed the guitar case. She laid it on her bed and unsnapped the latches, the mellow aroma of polished wood filling her senses. She noticed at once that the top string had broken. She ran a thumbnail across the remaining five, garishly out of tune yet surprisingly rich in tone. The reverberation hummed in her ears.

"Your timing is off. Play it again, Filipa."

"Are you deaf to your own tone quality? That chord twanged like a dying goose!"

"Get out, get out, get out! Don't waste my time again until you can play the adagio perfectly."

Filipa clamped her teeth together, the voices reminding her all over again why she would never, ever go back to music school. Angry tears filled her eyes. She slammed the lid shut and shoved the case into the farthest corner of the closet.

Ten minutes later she was knocking on Nathan's door.

"Hey, Fil. Been waiting for you." Showing her in, he moved his laptop from the sofa to the coffee table. "I was just going over some stuff I'm working on for this show-and-tell thing."

She forced a smile into her voice. "How's it going?"

"Three of the business people I've contacted so far, including the equipment rental guy, have accepted the invitation to come out next Saturday morning in time for the last class. We'll serve them a catered lunch afterward and do our little presentation."

"That's wonderful, Nathan. I know this is going to work."

"If it does, it's all thanks to you." He scooted in close beside her on the sofa.

Filipa gave a doubtful smirk. "I haven't done anything except make a lot of noise at the meeting."

"Oh, you've done plenty, Miss Beltran."

Giving her head a tiny shake, she looked away and hoped he wouldn't notice the tremor in her lower lip.

Nathan placed a finger under her chin and turned her face toward his. "What's wrong?"

She shrugged. "Just going slightly insane trying to figure out my life."

"Hmmm, sounds like my cue to turn on my sensitive side." Nathan shifted sideways, one arm resting along the back of the sofa behind her head. "Zo, now you must tell Dr. Zigmund everyzing. Vere vould you like to begin?"

Filipa laughed in spite of herself—one more reason Nathan had stolen her heart. She heaved a resigned sigh. "How about the day I dropped out of school, packed my things, and headed home from New York?"

Turning serious, Nathan toyed with a strand of her hair. "I've been waiting for months for you to open up to me about that."

"It isn't that I haven't wanted to. But these past several weeks, working here at the farm, getting involved with the therapy classes, spending time with you . . . It's given me a lot to think about. Pastor Wolfe's sermon this morning was the icing on the cake."

"He did kind of lay it on the line about using our gifts."

Filipa tensed. "Ever since my first piano lesson, everyone's told me music is my gift. I was good and I knew it, and for years I didn't mind the long hours of practice. Then when my audition earned a scholarship to such a prestigious music school, my parents were the proudest people on the planet. I went to New York with huge aspirations, convinced I'd be the next John Williams or Julian Bream."

Nathan scratched his head. "Sorry, those names don't mean anything to me."

"Only two of the greatest classical guitarists ever." Filipa rolled her eyes.

"So what changed?"

She drew a deep breath and searched for words. "Somewhere along the way, my dreams of making beautiful music turned into something ugly. Distorted. Meaningless. The compulsion for perfection strangled the joy."

"And you don't think you can get it back?"

"I don't even know if I want to try." She cast Nathan a searching glance. "Since I've been helping here at Cross Roads Farm, I've realized my music wasn't serving anyone's interests but my own—unless you count my professors' egos and my parents' pride," she added with a huff. "But working with the kids and horses, seeing what a difference this place makes in their lives, *that's* something truly worthwhile. Far more so than mastering a difficult piece of music or getting a standing ovation at a concert."

Nathan faced forward and crossed his arms. He gnawed his lower lip. "You're making this too black and white, Fil. Yeah, you might have gotten your priorities slightly skewed, but you can't arbitrarily declare your musical gift worthless. God gave it to you for a reason."

She leapt from the sofa and spun around. "Can't you see that's exactly why I'm so confused? How can God want me to use a gift that no longer brings even a shred of joy or fulfillment—to me or anyone else?"

Rising, Nathan took her in his arms, and she melted against his chest. Resuming his flaky foreign accent, he said, "Eez time to end today's session. Dr. Zigmund must give zees furzer zought." Then he planted a kiss on top of her head and added in his normal voice, "I promise you, Fil, we'll figure this out."

Chapter Thirteen

The following Wednesday morning, Nathan and Sheridan met in the study to review the schedule for Saturday's show-and-tell. Perusing the spreadsheet open on his laptop, Nathan massaged his temple with one finger. "Our guests should all be here in time for the eleven a.m. class. Kingsley Station will deliver lunch at eleven thirty."

Sheridan followed along on her desktop computer. "Bev and I will set out the luncheon in the dining room while class is going on."

"Then after lunch we take them into the living room and do our thing." Nathan shot his sister a desperate frown. "And hopefully convince them to get behind us with their support."

"It'll work, Nathan. Once they've viewed a class and listened to personal stories from parents, clients, and a couple of our most dedicated volunteers, they'll whip out their checkbooks."

Kip strode into the room and stood behind Sheridan's chair, palms resting on her shoulders. "You guys ever gonna quit? My belly's sayin' lunchtime."

Seizing her husband's hand, Sheridan drew him forward for a quick kiss. "Honey, you were a bachelor for how long? I thought by now you'd surely know how to make yourself a sandwich."

"Yeah, but it tastes so much better when you make it for me." Kip spun Sheridan's chair around and pulled her to her feet, straight into his arms. With a soft chuckle, he nuzzled her neck.

Grinning, Nathan closed his laptop. "No need to spell it out—meeting adjourned."

Sheridan's mouth quirked in an apologetic smile. "Want to have a sandwich with us? We can talk more over lunch."

"No, thanks. Three is obviously a crowd." Nathan rose to leave. "Anyway, I think we covered everything we needed to."

He wouldn't let the lovebirds see how envious their happiness made him, how it only deepened his longing for a similar happiness with Filipa. Ambling across the lawn toward the cottage, he turned his attention to another item on his personal agenda, something he'd been itching to look into all week.

Shoes off, feet propped up on the coffee table, he opened his computer again and ran an internet search for Filipa's music school. Other than the name and location, he knew very little about the place. Though he and Fil had emailed fairly often when she'd first gone to New York, as they both became more and more enmeshed in their studies, keeping up with each other became a lesser priority.

A mistake Nathan sorely regretted now. If they'd stayed in touch, maybe he'd have realized early on what the pressure was doing to Fil. Maybe he could have helped somehow, before she completely burned out.

He scrolled through the school's website, learning all he could about the faculty, curriculum, music disciplines offered, degree plans, and general philosophy. On the surface, everything about the school was impressive, from the distinguished faculty to the long list of alumni who'd earned high honors in the music world.

But the further Nathan read—and the more he read between the lines—the more uncomfortable he became. In the subtle word choices, in the "candid" photographs, even in the carefully structured arrangement of each web page, he could now see exactly what Filipa had described: perfectionism permeated the entire program.

Perfection as an ideal was one thing. "Be perfect, therefore, as your heavenly Father is perfect," Jesus said, but Nathan felt pretty sure God never intended for His children to sacrifice their uniqueness to become mindless, expressionless robots focused only on rules and technique.

He could only imagine how stifled Filipa must have felt in such a learning environment. If he could find a way to get her into the *right* kind of program, one that nourished creativity and artistic expression, he felt certain she'd find her joy again.

And as much as he wanted to do this for Filipa's sake, he had a selfish reason as well. She needed to fall in love with music all over again before she'd ever allow herself to fall in love with Nathan.

"Thanks for coming, Mr. Gill. Cross Roads Farm really appreciates your support." Nathan shook hands with the rental company manager as they said their goodbyes on the front porch.

"My pleasure. You've completely sold me on the importance of the work you're doing here. Let me know if there's anything else you need." With a nod, the manager strode across the lawn toward his parked car.

Returning to the living room, Nathan collapsed into the nearest chair. "We did it!"

"I'll say." Sheridan fanned herself with the donation checks they'd just collected. "These will go a long way toward covering our out-of-pocket expenses for the cook-off. Plus Mr. Gill is letting us use all the tables and chairs we need rent-free."

Kip entered from the kitchen. "Ryan just left. I told him he could take a couple slices of pie home as payment for services rendered."

"He did a great job." Sheridan sank lower into an easy chair and stretched out her legs. "When he shared his story about what a messed-up kid he was and how our program helped turn him around, I thought I actually saw two of those buttoned-down businessmen tear up."

Footsteps pounded down the staircase, and a moment later Grace skidded around the corner. Gasping for breath, she shot her brother a panicked look. "Ryan's gone already?"

"Had to get to work," Kip said. "Which is what you and I need to be doin', little sister. It's deworming day." Pinching Grace's neck, he marched her toward the back door.

Nathan shared an exhausted look with Sheridan. "Not sure which is harder—deworming a horse, or convincing reluctant business owners to loosen their purse strings."

"Given the choice, I'd take deworming a horse." Sheridan heaved herself from the chair. "Guess I'd better tackle the kitchen cleanup."

"I'll give you a hand." Rising, Nathan shrugged out of his sports coat and draped it across the arm of a chair.

Within an hour they'd cleared the dining room table, tossed the trash, and loaded the dishwasher. After adding detergent, Sheridan selected the wash cycle. As the dishwasher hummed, she poured herself a glass of iced tea and then pulled out a chair. "So how are things with you and Filipa?"

Nathan filled a glass for himself while carefully avoiding eye contact. "Things?"

"Don't play dumb with me. It's obvious you two have become a lot more than just friends."

He sat across from his sister and placed his iced tea glass on the table. "It's kind of like you and Kip. You knew you were in love with him way before he was ready to admit his feelings."

Sheridan cast him a sad smile. "Oh, honey, I'm sorry. I know how frustrated you must feel."

"It's not just frustration. It's . . . anger." Nathan's stomach muscles knotted. "I've been doing some digging. This music school she was going to—it's all wrong for her."

"But isn't it one of the best?"

"It's true, they turn out some of the most skilled musicians in the country. But their teaching methods, their program structure—it sucked the life out of her." He described to Sheridan some of the things he'd found online.

Sheridan drew her lower lip between her teeth. "I remember Filipa as a little girl, how creative and spontaneous she was. Then to follow her dream only to lose it to performance-focused autocrats . . ."

Nathan traced a finger through the frosty condensation on his glass. "I have to do something, Sher. I'm going to find a way to fix this."

"How?" Suspicion colored Sheridan's tone.

"I'm working on some ideas, putting out some feelers." Nathan mentally reviewed the list of music schools he'd compiled over the past few days. There had to be one where Filipa would thrive, where her natural gifts would be nurtured, not forced into someone else's mold.

"I know you love her, Nathan, but be careful." Sheridan reached for her brother's arm. "You can't 'fix things' for her like you would balance a budget or run a committee meeting."

Pushing up from his chair, he shot his sister an indignant frown. "I thought you of all people would understand. I only want to help."

Still half asleep, Filipa carried her bowl of cold cereal to the table. Only the faintest traces of morning light cut through the darkness beyond the kitchen window. The weatherman had promised a sunny start to the week—a welcome change after a miserably cold, wet Sunday.

At least they'd had good weather for the show-and-tell at Cross Roads Farm on Saturday. Nathan had sounded extremely pleased when he'd called that afternoon to share the results.

The only disadvantage to all these fundraising efforts was that Nathan's work kept him busier than ever, and Filipa couldn't help missing him.

A shuffling sound drew her attention to the doorway. "Papa?" She stared in surprise, her spoon poised halfway between bowl and mouth. "What are you doing up this early?"

"I am going to work with you." Her father reached into the cupboard for another cereal bowl.

Filipa narrowed her gaze. "Did I miss something? As in, your doctor's permission?"

"Were you not there at my appointment last week?" Shooting her a disbelieving frown, Papa filled his bowl with raisin and wheat flake cereal. "You heard him say I am well enough to resume most normal activity."

The next bite of cereal stuck in Filipa's throat. She washed it down with a sip of hot coffee. "Yes, but I doubt he'd consider mucking stalls *normal activity*."

"You will muck. I will supervise." Setting down his bowl and a mug of coffee, her father took his seat. "The exercise will be good for both my knee and my heart."

Obviously it was no use arguing. Filipa finished her breakfast in silence, but inside, her emotions collided. She should be praising God for her father's rapid recovery. Growing stronger every day, he'd experienced no complications from either the knee replacement or the heart attack.

On the other hand, Papa's ability to return to work meant Filipa might soon be unemployed again, and then where would she be? Back to filling out applications and trying to fit her "square peg" skills into "round hole" job descriptions.

At least she was in a different place both mentally and spiritually than she'd been last summer. She understood herself a little better, and she'd come to realize what had been missing for so long. Whatever path she took, she'd trust God to lead her toward something meaningful, worthwhile, and brimming with joy.

Determined to claim a little more of that joy right now, Filipa mustered a smile as she grabbed a jacket and hurried her father out to the pickup. How could she forget the fun she used to have tagging after Papa while he worked? She'd probably gotten in the way more often than she actually helped, but he'd never complained—much, anyway.

And Papa hadn't minded when she'd sneak into the hayloft to sing silly songs accompanied by the cheap ukulele he'd picked up for her at a garage sale. By age twelve she'd graduated from the ukulele to her first guitar, another garage sale find. The tone quality left a lot to be desired, but back then Filipa hadn't known any better. All she cared about was making music.

It wasn't long afterward that her middle school music teacher noticed her natural abilities. Knowing the Beltrans couldn't afford private music lessons, Mrs. Smith offered to teach Filipa in exchange for helping in the classroom. Twice a week, Filipa stayed after school for a half-hour of piano and a half-hour of guitar lessons. Those days, filled with encouragement, laughter, and affirmation, held some of Filipa's happiest memories.

Dear God, if I could just get those feelings back!

With her dad pitching in, the morning chores went quickly. She made sure he didn't overextend himself, but she couldn't stop his not-so-subtle critiques of her routine.

"Need I remind you I've been doing fine here by myself for weeks now?" Filipa tromped out of the barn with another cartful of manure and soiled shavings.

Papa marched along beside her toward the collection bin. "And must I remind you I have worked at Cross Roads Farm since you were in grade school?"

She angled him an annoyed frown. "Then, of course, you're the expert. Excuse me for being so presumptuous."

Reaching the collection bin behind the garage, Filipa emptied the cart, then started back to the barn. She and her father were still bickering when Nathan stepped out of the cottage, laptop tucked under his arm.

He stopped in the middle of the lane. "Manuelo! Didn't expect to see you around here so soon. How's the knee?"

"Better every day." He shot Filipa a glare. "Which is a good thing since my lazy daughter refuses to listen to the voice of experience and do things my way."

Filipa released the cart handles. The rear supports hit the ground with a clatter. "So now it's your way or the highway? Give me some credit, will you? I'm not entirely brainless."

Nathan gaped. "What is up with you two? You're worse than Fred and Ethel in an *I Love Lucy* rerun."

Only then did Filipa realize how catty she sounded. She stared at the ground. "Sorry, guess I'm a little irritable."

"A *little*?"

"Okay, a lot." She gripped the cart handles again. "I should get back to work."

"Filipa." Her father halted her with his noisy sigh. "You are doing a fine job in my place. I am grateful and should not have been so critical."

She could only nod as she continued toward the barn.

Minutes later, as she set to work on the next stall, footsteps sounded in the aisle. The stride was too long and purposeful to be her father's. She glanced out the stall door to see Nathan frowning at her, fists planted on his hipbones.

He hiked a brow. "Having a bad day, huh?"

"Oh, Nathan." Filipa leaned the pitchfork against the wall, suddenly wanting nothing more than to nestle into the shelter of his arms. But she knew she smelled like a manure pile, and Nathan looked as if he'd just showered and shaved. She tucked her hands into her pockets with a shrug.

"I sent your dad into the house to have a cup of coffee with Kip and Sheridan." He offered his hand. "Wanna take a walk?"

She smirked. "Boss's orders?"

"Boss's orders."

With a reluctant sigh, she took his hand. On their way out of the barn, she noticed his laptop lying on a tack trunk. "Are you sure you don't have something more important you should be doing?"

"Nothing's more important than keeping my employees happy. So fess up. Why so grumpy?"

"Same old same old. When Papa informed me he was coming with me this morning, it reminded me this job is only temporary." She kicked a pebble. "Which means I'm running out of time to figure out what happens next."

"I wouldn't sweat it. Things have a way of working out." Nathan looped his arm around Filipa's shoulders and tugged her off balance.

"Hey!" She fell hard against his side but couldn't deny that having his arm around her felt pretty good. Steady. Sure. Solid.

She halted abruptly, this time pulling him off balance. When he looked at her in confusion, she slid her arms around his waist and rested her head upon his chest. Beneath his cottony pullover, his heart thumped out a reassuring rhythm. She burrowed deeper into his embrace. "I want this, Nathan, I really do."

Grasping her by the shoulders, he gently freed himself to cup her face in his hands. "What, Fil? What do you want?"

"You . . . us . . ." The words caught in her throat.

"Then just say it, Fil. Say you love me. Because I know you do." Lips parted, eyelids lowered, he angled his head and drew closer. His mouth found hers, and she drank in the warm, cinnamon-tasting freshness of his kiss.

Senses reeling, she pulled away far sooner than she wanted to. Every nerve hummed, and she gasped for oxygen as if she'd just run a marathon. Forcing down a swallow, she clutched his hands. "I do love you, Nathan. I wish it were this easy, but—"

"Don't say it." He enfolded her against his chest once more, chin resting atop her head. "I know you've still got stuff to work out, but we can do it together. Let me help you, Fil. Let me be there for you in every way that counts."

She clung to him, wanting with all her heart to abandon herself to his love. Could it be God had brought her back to Cross Roads Farm just so she and Nathan could find each other again? If it took turning her back on music to rediscover everything she'd sacrificed, to find the love she'd always longed for, then nothing else mattered. She'd find her joy right here in Nathan's arms.

Chapter Fourteen

"Sounds great. Let me look into it and I'll get back to you." Clicking off his cell phone, Nathan strode down the hallway toward the study, where Sheridan waited for his help to work out Saturday's volunteer schedule.

Reaching the study door, he heard Sheridan on a phone conversation of her own, so he leaned against the opposite wall to wait. As the call dragged on—definitely fundraiser-related, so Nathan wasn't about to interrupt—he let his gaze roam the array of photographs and pithy sayings that had adorned the hallway since he was a kid.

With time and familiarity he'd almost stopped noticing the decor, but today one piece of art jumped out at him—a small print featuring a monarch butterfly, and beneath it the words, *If you love something, let it go.*

If Nathan needed any reassurance he was doing the right thing, he'd just found it.

"Hey, you." Sheridan stood in the doorway. "Gonna stand there daydreaming or help me with the schedule?"

Nathan pushed away from the wall. "Sorry, just thinking."

"You looked like you were a million miles away. Fundraiser stuff? Or maybe . . ." Her lips curled into an impish smile. "Yep, you were thinking about Fil."

Nathan's face warmed. He couldn't suppress a grin. "Like I never catch you mooning over your cowboy. Does the honeymoon *ever* end?"

"Not if I can help it!" With a giggle, Sheridan fisted a handful of Nathan's shirt front and dragged him into the study. "Time to focus, lover boy. We've got work to do."

An hour later, Nathan had laid out not only the Saturday volunteer schedule but the following week's as well. Judging by the grateful sigh Sheridan gusted out, he figured he'd just saved her a full day's work and the headaches that would have gone along with it.

She leaned back in her chair and propped one foot on the corner of the desk, wiggling her toes against the end of a pink argyle sock. "Don't forget, you promised after the cook-off you'd find a way to make this scheduling business less of an ordeal."

"Workin' on it, sis." Nathan raised his arms overhead for a good, long stretch. "I was thinking maybe you'd like to get your instructor certification. With the client waiting list growing, we've been talking about adding a class day."

Sheridan's eyes sparkled. "I'd love working directly with the kids again. But who'd take over the client and volunteer scheduling? You sure can't do everything."

"Peggy Abbott has a great head for organization. I'm thinking of hiring her part-time."

Sheridan cast him a doubtful glance. "Are we ready— financially, I mean—to make a change like that?"

"If this fundraiser brings in as much as I'm projecting, I think we can do it."

"You're the business whiz." Sheridan lowered her foot

to the floor and sat up. "Which reminds me, Mr. Marlin phoned earlier with a reminder to start pulling stuff together for the tax return."

Scowling, Nathan slapped his forehead. "I haven't had time to even think about taxes."

"Guess you'd better. April fifteenth isn't that far away." Rising, Sheridan glanced at her wristwatch. "My, would you look at the time! I'm late for, um, grocery shopping or something!"

"Chicken." Nathan slapped at her arm as she darted past.

No sense putting it off any longer. And how hard could it be? Mr. Marlin had been the family's CPA for years, so all Nathan had to do was pull together all the relevant statements, receipts, and business records, and Mr. Marlin would do the rest.

Settling in behind the desk with last year's return and supporting documents, Nathan gave the thick stack of pages a thorough perusal. Awhile later, armed with a list of documentation he needed to locate, he returned to the filing cabinet and started digging.

Except he wasn't liking what he *wasn't* finding. The files had been in pretty good shape last fall when Nathan's mother first turned things over to him. But since then, it appeared Nathan had entrusted way too much of the filing to Sheridan. Credit card bills were stuck behind utility bills. A client record somehow found its way into an invoice folder.

Great. Just great. Yep, definitely time to get Sheridan out from behind the desk and into the arena working with kids, where her real gifts lay.

"Where is it, where is it?" Nathan riffled through several file folders in search of a missing receipt. There *had* to be a record of the roof repair they'd done on the barn after last spring's hailstorm.

He'd worked his way through several folders when he noticed a manila envelope wedged at the very back of the bottom file drawer. He tugged the envelope free, then undid the metal clasp and peered inside. The contents appeared to be a random assortment of letters and receipts, none of them recent. Curious, Nathan spread the papers across the desk.

Immediately he recognized his father's sprawling cursive—signatures at the bottom of invoices, handwritten notes attached to copies of letters on Cross Roads Farm stationery. On closer inspection, Nathan realized these all related to gifts or charitable donations, some dating back fifteen or twenty years. Dad had once given $10,000 to Kingsley Faith Fellowship's building fund, paid $2,000 toward a former client's medical bills, supplied $3,500 worth of household goods and school supplies for an overseas mission team.

Wow, Dad, I always knew you were a generous man. I just had no idea how generous!

The next sheet of paper Nathan unfolded made his heart race—a receipt for $5,000 paid to a New York music store. Stapled to the receipt was a copy of a letter Nathan's father had written to the manager, which read in part:

Thanks for your discretion, Mr. James. Neither Miss Beltran nor anyone in her family must ever learn who provided this gift. I trust you will assist Miss Beltran in selecting one of your finest guitars, an instrument that will best showcase her exceptional musical talent and serve her well for many years to come.

Nathan's hand went limp, the letter falling into his lap as he sagged into the chair. His *father* had provided the money for Filipa's guitar? Nathan still remembered Fil's excitement when she'd emailed him about the anonymous donor who had made it possible for her to purchase the guitar of her dreams.

That settled it. Whatever it took, whatever it cost, Nathan would make sure Filipa didn't give up on her music.

"I don't argue, ma'am—it's a fine instrument." The man behind the counter—his name tag read "Jake"—stroked his graying goatee. "But I can't pay you nearly what it's worth. I have to make a profit, too, you understand."

Filipa masked a disappointed sigh. She'd already visited two other reputable guitar shops in the Charlotte area, only to receive similar responses. "What's the most you could give me?"

Jake plucked a string, fingered a fret. "Needs a bit of work. You haven't played it in a while, have you?" His lips skewed. "Two grand, maybe twenty-two fifty. Best I can do."

She closed the lid on the case. "Thanks. I need to think about it." The decision to sell her Paulino Bernabe hadn't come easily, but doing so seemed the logical next step in getting on with her life. Since she no longer had any intention of pursuing a music career, holding on to the guitar seemed pointless—even more so now that she'd chosen to give her heart fully to Nathan. His love meant everything to her. His laughter was the only music she needed.

"Be happy to restring it for you and get it playable again," Jake said. "You must be pretty good to own a guitar of this caliber."

Filipa offered him a sad-eyed smile. "I am—or at least I was," she said, not bragging, just an honest statement of fact.

Jake rested one hand on the neck of the case, his thumb grazing the hard-shell covering. "If I were hurting for cash, I'd sooner sign away my house than part with a masterpiece like this."

"Not even an option, since I'm currently living with my parents." Filipa closed her fingers around the guitar case handle. "Thanks for your time."

Jake tightened his hold on the case. "Leave it with me, okay? Let me restore it to playing condition for you. It's a sin to let this instrument languish in the back of a closet or under a bed."

Guilty as charged. Had he seen the longing in her eyes, the aching hunger that filled her every time she opened that case? *Dear God, I do want to play again—so badly it hurts!*

She inched the case across the counter but didn't release the handle. "How much would it cost?"

The man didn't speak for several long seconds. The only sound was the occasional twang coming from the workroom in back. Finally Jake leaned toward her, propping his elbows atop the case. "I have a granddaughter who'd love to learn guitar, but I haven't had the time or the patience to teach her. A month or two of lessons would easily cover fixing up this beauty."

Filipa nibbled the inside of her lip. Although she'd never much enjoyed tutoring egotistical guitar students, she certainly had plenty of experience. "How old is she?"

"Eleven . . . and there's something else." His gaze flicked sideways for a moment. "She has Down syndrome."

A sudden lift of her heart took Filipa by surprise. She remembered the Down syndrome client she'd worked with a few times at Cross Roads Farm. Even more, she recalled the sense of fulfillment she'd experienced being part of a team that helped such children achieve new goals.

She pushed the case to Jake's side of the counter. "When can I meet your granddaughter?"

Ten minutes later she left the shop with directions to the girl's home for a get-acquainted meeting that afternoon and an appointment for their first lesson the following Monday. The lessons would be a bit of a drive since the girl's family lived on the outskirts of Charlotte, but with careful scheduling, Filipa could easily drop her father off at his physical therapy appointment on the way, then return in plenty of time to pick him up.

Arriving for her visit with the girl and her mother, Filipa felt even more encouraged. Debby Hunter bubbled and bounced with excitement, proudly showing Filipa the three-quarter-size guitar her grandfather had given her for Christmas.

"Can you teach me something right now?" Debby's round eyes sparkled.

"Well, let's see." Filipa sat on the sofa next to the girl and took the guitar into her own lap. "Here's a song with three easy chords. It's one of the very first things I learned to play." Careful to demonstrate proper finger placement, Filipa strummed each chord in succession, then sang along as she played "Blowin' in the Wind."

When she finished, Debby clapped and squealed. "Now show me how!"

Amazingly, the girl caught on quickly. Her chords were

far from crisp, but her enthusiasm more than made up for what she lacked in technique. She was still strumming away when Debby's mother showed Filipa to the door at the end of the visit.

Mrs. Hunter followed Filipa out to the front step and pulled the door closed behind them. "You have no idea what this means to Debby. She's reaching the age when she's more aware than ever of her differentness. To have someone with your talent take an interest in her . . . it's such a boost for her self-esteem."

Filipa's throat ached. She hugged her purse against her chest. "Mrs. Hunter, you have no idea what coming here today has meant for *me.*"

If there was one trait Nathan wished he'd never inherited from his dad, it was his stupid cowlick. He plastered it down with a spritz of styling spray and hoped it would hold until after he kissed Fil good night at the end of their date.

Date. Finally he could call it that! A leisurely dinner at an upscale Charlotte restaurant, a romantic movie with (hopefully) lots of snuggling in the darkened theater, a slow drive home, and a whole lot more kissing and snuggling before they said good night at her front door.

Yes!

He arrived at the Beltran home to a much different reception than the last time he'd picked up Filipa for an evening out. A warmly smiling Rosa Beltran invited him to have a seat in their cozy living room. "You look especially handsome tonight, Nathan. Filipa will be ready in a moment. Would you like some iced tea while you wait?"

"Uh, no, thanks. I'm fine." He started toward the sofa, where Joseph and Elisa sat watching TV.

Manuelo started to rise from his plush recliner. "Take my chair. It is much more comfortable."

"No, really, keep your seat." Nathan resisted the urge to loosen his collar. *Something* was definitely going on here. He made a beeline for the sofa and plopped down next to the kids before Rosa or Manuelo offered to give him a foot massage or promised him their firstborn child or—

Wait. Their firstborn child was *exactly* the prize he sought!

Joseph sniffed and wrinkled his nose. "You smell like vanilla ice cream."

"It's my aftershave." Nathan arched a brow. "You got something against vanilla ice cream?"

"I love vanilla ice cream. But I wouldn't *wear* it."

"Now, Joseph . . ." Rosa's warning glare morphed into an apologetic smile as she looked toward Nathan. She propped a hip on the arm of her husband's chair. Her voice fell to nearly a whisper. "Our Filipa has seemed so much happier these past few days. You are good for her, Nathan. We are grateful."

Heat roared up Nathan's neck. If not for the two kids sitting next to him, he might be tempted to tell Manuelo and Rosa how he really felt about their daughter, maybe even get all old-fashioned and ask their permission to officially court her.

Then the object of his dreams emerged from the back bedroom. Her eyes lit up when she met Nathan's gaze. "Hey, you."

"Hey, yourself." He stood, forgetting anyone else was in the room. "You look crazy-beautiful."

A barfing sound at Nathan's right reminded him they were definitely *not* alone.

"Joseph!" Rosa leaped up. She pinched her young son's ear and dragged him off toward the kitchen.

Filipa rolled her eyes as she strode to her father's chair. She bent to kiss the top of his head. "Don't wait up, Papa. I have my key."

Manuelo wiggled his eyebrows. "If I fall asleep in my chair, *no es importante*."

"If you fall asleep in your chair, you did it on purpose." Filipa reached for Nathan's hand. "Let's go before my family totally embarrasses us—again."

As they walked out to the car, Nathan stopped her in the driveway for a quick kiss, his fingers getting lost in her mass of silky black hair. He tilted his head back and searched her face. "Your mom was right. You do seem happier lately."

With a shy smile, she lowered her gaze. "I guess I am."

"Any special reason?"

Fingering his lapel, she peered up at him through thick, dark lashes. "Do I need one besides you?"

"Oooh, baby, you sure know how to stroke a guy's ego!" Puffing out his chest, Nathan helped her into the car.

As he climbed in behind the wheel, he squeezed Filipa's hand, and the loving look in her eyes nearly undid him. How had he ever deserved a woman like her? Beautiful, talented, tenderhearted, she was everything he'd ever wanted.

But this plan he'd been working on—he must be totally out of his mind. The answer he'd been waiting for had arrived in an email late yesterday, and now the printout was burning a hole in his breast pocket. He'd thought about springing the news on Filipa over dinner . . . but maybe not.

He'd rather enjoy their time together, unspoiled by any talk of fundraisers or music school or anything else. Tonight would be all about showing Fil how much he loved her, how deeply he longed to spend the rest of his life showing her exactly how much.

Because, if things went according to plan, it could be a long, long time before he'd have this chance again.

Yes, he was certifiably insane.

Still glowing after her amazing date with Nathan, then a lazy picnic in Kingsley Park after church on Sunday, Filipa now looked forward to her first real guitar lesson with Debby. She wasn't exactly certain why she hadn't told Nathan or her parents about her new guitar student. Maybe because she was still getting used to the idea, herself.

"Papa, we need to go." She checked her purse for keys and cell phone.

"Coming, *mija*." Papa emerged from the bathroom, his thinning hair slicked down and shiny. "Why such a big hurry? We have time yet."

"You don't want to be late for your appointment. There could be traffic."

Donning his windbreaker, Filipa's father made a rumbling noise in his throat. "In all these weeks I do not recall a single time when traffic was a problem on Monday afternoon."

"You never know. Why take chances?"

Angling his daughter a glare, Papa held the door for her.

"If I did not know better, I would think you were in a rush to meet your sweetheart."

"Papa!" Filipa bustled out the door and marched to the pickup. "I just need to take care of some . . . errands. Anyway, Nathan's hard at work this afternoon." As usual. Her only glimpse of him that morning had been when she passed by his cottage window on her way to and from the manure bin. Each time, he'd either been hunched over his laptop or engrossed in a phone call.

As they drove up the highway toward Charlotte, Papa flexed his knee a few times and then cleared his throat. "It will not be much longer until I can return to work."

"I know, Papa." Filipa sighed as she changed lanes to pass a big, yellow moving truck. "You'll need to start back gradually, though. We can work together awhile yet."

"Still, it is not too soon to consider what you will do when I no longer need your help."

Filipa aimed a crooked smile her father's way. "Don't worry about me, Papa. I'm trusting God for direction now, and I know He'll come through."

Her father touched her arm, and she glimpsed the hopeful look in his eyes. "Dare I hope the Lord is nudging my precious daughter back to her music?"

Giving her head a tiny shake, she cast a glance heavenward. "I'll keep you posted, okay?"

Seemingly satisfied, Filipa's father moved on to less complicated topics. After dropping him off at the PT center, she drove on into Charlotte to the guitar shop to pick up her Paulino Bernabe. Jake had promised it would be ready in time for Debby Hunter's lesson.

Twenty minutes later, when Mrs. Hunter showed Filipa into the family room, Filipa sucked in a gasp to find not only Debby but three other children as well, each with the round face and upturned eyes so typical of Down syndrome.

And all the children looked toward Filipa with eager expressions and guitars on their laps.

"I should have called to let you know," Mrs. Hunter said, her tone soft and apologetic, "but this was all pretty last-minute. Debby couldn't resist telling her special-ed classmates about you, and the next thing I knew, the moms were phoning this afternoon asking if their kids could have lessons, too."

Filipa glanced around the room, a nervous flutter tickling her chest. *A whole class of guitar students?*

"I know you have an arrangement with my dad to teach Debby," Mrs. Hunter continued, "but the other parents will pay the going rate." She handed Filipa three checks. "I hope this is enough for today."

Filipa could hardly find her voice. "Th–thank you. This is fine—more than enough."

Debby waved excitedly. "I can play my song, Miss Fi-fip-flipia!"

Still stunned, Filipa chuckled as she tucked the checks into her purse. "Why don't you call me Miss Fil?"

Debby strummed the chords to "Blowin' in the Wind" with firm, noisy strokes, alternating between singing the words she remembered and humming the rest.

When the song ended, Filipa applauded, as did Mrs. Hunter and the other children. "That's excellent, Debby! I'm so proud of you."

Mrs. Hunter laughed. "She's been practicing every spare minute since you were here last week. Her dad and I are sincerely hoping you'll be expanding her repertoire very soon."

Filipa lifted a hand to her throat. "As quickly as she learned that song, you have nothing to worry about."

"Are you sure you're okay with teaching the other kids?" Mrs. Hunter asked with an imploring smile.

Taking in each grinning, wide-eyed face, Filipa inhaled deeply. "Oh, yeah. More than okay."

"Then I'll let you get started." Mrs. Hunter took Filipa's jacket and purse. "I'll be in the kitchen. If you need anything at all, just let me know."

Filipa felt everyone's eyes on her as she settled into a straight-backed chair in the center of the room. Laying the guitar case at her feet, she unsnapped the latches and eased back the lid. As she lifted the Paulino Bernabe into her lap, every nerve pulsed with anticipation. The polished surface gleamed with renewed luster, the subtle scents of spruce and rosewood rising to meet her. Gently she ran her thumb across the strings, each note resounding in perfect tune.

Out of habit Filipa rested the curve of the guitar upon her left thigh, but as she started to raise the headstock to eye level in the classical position, she remembered these were beginning students. In one subtle movement she shifted the guitar to her right leg and lowered the neck into a more relaxed hold. "Okay, kids, ready to learn some chords?"

"Yes!"

The cacophony that followed for the next forty-five minutes brought tears of laughter to Filipa's eyes more than once. In all her years of music study she'd never encountered such eager students. Helping them find their fingering and learn simple strumming patterns carried her back to her own childhood and the simple joy of making music.

This is how it was always supposed to be, isn't it, Lord?

When the lesson ended, Debby insisted, "Now you play something for us, Miss Fil."

"I'm a little rusty, but I'll try." Calluses long gone, Filipa's fingertips already burned, but with her young audience nodding their encouragement, she'd endure the pain.

Recalling the piece that had so moved her the night she'd turned on the radio for Jet, she shifted the guitar into classical hold and began to play *Recuerdos de la Alhambra* with more warmth and passion than she'd known in years.

When the last note died away, the room stood in silence. Filipa opened her eyes to see four sets of eyes aglow with wonder.

Mrs. Hunter stood in the kitchen doorway, breathless. "I've never heard anything so beautiful in my life."

Swallowing the lump in her throat, Filipa smiled her thanks as she lowered the guitar into its case.

Only then did she notice the blood seeping from three of her fingertips.

"Oh, honey!" Mrs. Hunter reached for Filipa's wrist and pulled her up from the chair. Leading her into the kitchen, she gave Filipa a knowing frown. "You haven't played in a while, have you?"

"Not since last summer." Filipa sucked air between her teeth as Mrs. Hunter thrust her fingers under cold running water in the kitchen sink.

"Why? Was it an injury? Illness?"

"Nothing like that." Accepting the paper towel Mrs. Hunter offered, Filipa dried her hands, then wrapped her fingers in the damp towel. "I just . . . burned out."

"But you play so beautifully. You should be on a concert stage." The woman nodded toward the family room, where raucous guitar chords twanged as the children practiced their new skills. "I can't even imagine what a step down this must be for you."

"Oh, no, Mrs. Hunter." Tears filled Filipa's eyes. "This is the biggest step *up* I've taken in a long, long time."

"That about wraps up our business for tonight." Nathan perused the meeting agenda one last time. "Anyone have anything to add before we adjourn?"

Bev Williams spoke up. "Just that you've done an outstanding job pulling all this together and keeping us organized. It's going to be a fantastic event, Nathan."

Chest warming with pride, Nathan slid his notes into a soft-sided briefcase. "Sure couldn't do this without everyone's help. You're a great team to work with."

The cook-off was now barely a month away. Eight barbecue teams had registered, and over two hundred dinner tickets had already been sold, the scope of the event expanding beyond Nathan's grandest expectations. The sponsor backing they'd garnered as a result of the show-and-tell and other personal contacts guaranteed Cross Roads Farm a sizable profit from the event. That money, combined with client tuition, grants, and donations, would easily see them through the next couple of years and allow the program growth Nathan and Sheridan wanted to see.

The committee members drifted out in twos and threes, busily chatting about what they needed to accomplish in the weeks ahead. Nathan went around the conference table pushing in chairs while Sheridan brushed away snack crumbs and Filipa erased the whiteboard.

With the room in order, Nathan tucked his briefcase under his arm. "You gals *finally* ready to head home?"

"More than ready!" Sheridan slipped her arms into her sweater sleeves.

"Me, too," Filipa said with a yawn. "I should have stayed home tonight. I think I dozed through half the meeting."

Nathan pinched the nape of her neck. "You trying to say my meetings are boring?"

"Not *your* meetings, O Great One. I hang on your every word!"

"Watch it, Fil." Sheridan nudged her with an elbow. "This guy's head is big enough already."

As they started out the door, Nathan tossed Sheridan his car keys. "We'll catch up," he said, his arm locked around Filipa. Reaching behind him, he flipped off the light switch in the meeting room.

Sheridan glanced over her shoulder with a smirk. "Uh, kids, do you need a chaperone?"

"Not on your life." Nathan drew Filipa back into the room and kicked the door partway closed.

"Nath—"

He silenced her with a long, lazy kiss. "Been wanting to do that all evening."

Her breathy sigh tickled his neck as she snuggled close. "Wow, you sure know how to wake a girl up."

"Why so tired tonight? Your boss working you too hard?" His lips grazed her temple. He buried his nose in the softness of her hair.

"No, it's . . ." With a subtle tremor she pulled away. "We shouldn't keep Sheridan waiting."

In the void she left behind, his chest felt hollow. He reached for her, trying to read her expression in the dim light from the corridor. "I'd rather stay here holding you."

She didn't resist when he pulled her back into his

arms and smothered her mouth with more kisses. He still could scarcely believe how much he loved her, needed her, wanted her. And he sensed her deepening love for him as she returned his kiss with a fervor that made his pulse race.

Her soft chuckle vibrated against his lips. Her palms crept up between them and pressed against his chest. "Nathan, we really have to go. It's late."

Later than you think, Fil. Later than you think.

Farm business and cook-off arrangements kept Nathan tied to his cell phone and computer for the next few days, but every time he saw Filipa pass his window, his gut pinched. It took every ounce of willpower to keep from tossing his laptop aside and rushing out to be with her. Shoveling manure, cleaning out water pails, grooming horses, whatever—as long as he could be close to the woman he loved.

Seeing Manuelo show up for work with his daughter with increasing frequency helped ease Nathan's mind about the plans he'd been working on. He knew Filipa would never agree to them as long as she felt she was needed at the farm.

He'd have to tell her soon.

His cell phone chimed. He snatched it off the end table and checked the Caller ID. Exactly the call he'd been waiting for. "Nathan Cross."

"Good morning. This is Janet Locker."

"Ms. Locker, thanks for your email last week. I can't tell you how grateful I am for your help." Nathan rose and walked to the window. Over in the arena, Filipa was setting up traffic cones and PVC pipes for the Thursday afternoon therapy classes.

"After everything you've told me, and especially after doing some checking on my own, I'm convinced our school will prove the ideal situation for your friend. I'm anxious to meet her in person and hear her play."

Nathan pumped a fist but kept his voice level. "So you're coming to Charlotte?"

"My flight arrives Monday at one fifteen. I'll only have that afternoon, though. I must catch a plane back to Baltimore first thing Tuesday morning."

"I understand." Nathan watched Filipa set down a cone and catch her breath before trudging toward the stack of PVC pipes. It would be such a relief to see her leave this drudgery behind and get back to her music again.

"I've reserved a room at the Sheraton. Could you bring Miss Beltran there on Monday afternoon, say around two thirty?"

"She'll be there. Thank you, Ms. Locker. Thank you from the bottom of my heart."

The call ended, and Nathan turned away from the window, one hand covering his eyes as realization forced the air from his lungs. He was doing the right thing, he felt certain—but would Filipa agree?

By the time classes ended Saturday morning, Filipa was hungry enough to start gnawing on the dressage saddle she carried to the tack room. She shoved it onto the rack, wincing as the leather chafed her tender fingertips. She'd tried all the old tricks to ease the blisters and toughen up her fingers again—soaking in ice water, scrubbing with an emery board, limiting practice time to only fifteen minutes at a stretch.

The hardest part had been finding a place to practice in secret. As much as she enjoyed teaching those precious children, she could do without the additional pressure sure to come from both her parents and Nathan if they knew she'd started playing her guitar again.

Finally, her only choice had been to confide in Sheridan, who let her keep her guitar in the upstairs guest room and go there to practice whenever time—and privacy concerns—permitted.

As Filipa turned to leave the tack room, Sheridan sidled in, huffing and puffing under the weight of a heavy Western saddle. Rushing over, Filipa grabbed one side. "Let me help."

"Thanks. I don't know where the big, strong guys disappear to around this time." Together they heaved the saddle onto an empty rack. Then Sheridan pushed her damp blond bangs off her forehead with a groan. After a quick glance over her shoulder, she murmured, "How's the practice going?"

Filipa extended her hands, palms facing up, and wiggled her fingers. "Better, but still painful."

"I'm so glad you're playing again. Have you decided when you're going to tell Nathan?"

The door burst open. "Tell me what?"

Filipa and Sheridan both jumped. Sheridan spun around and slugged her brother in the arm. "That you're a first-class creep for ducking out for a phone call at exactly the moment we needed help putting tack away."

"Can I help it if yet another barbecue team wants to sign up? No way I'm turning down those entry fees!" Nathan sidled over and tucked Filipa beneath his arm.

"While I was on the phone, I tossed a frozen pizza in the oven. Want to join me for lunch?"

"Pizza—you said the magic word!"

"You two go on," Sheridan said. "Kip will be out in a minute. He and I can finish up."

Filipa was too hungry to protest. "I owe you one, Sher." *Or two, or three . . .*

Stepping through Nathan's front door, Filipa caught the tantalizing aroma of pizza sauce and pepperoni. Her stomach rumbled.

Nathan looked at her askance. "Maybe I should have thrown in a couple more pizzas."

"Just stay out of my way, big boy, and I might save you a bite or two."

After washing up, Filipa set out paper plates, napkins, and frosty cans of cola while Nathan sliced the pizza. They sat elbow to elbow at the small, round dinette, Filipa wolfing down pizza as if she hadn't eaten in days. She battled Nathan for the last slice, which he finally conceded with a helpless laugh.

While she scraped up every last crumb from both her plate and the pizza pan, Nathan edged his chair back. "If you're through eating me out of house and home, there's something I want to talk to you about."

Filipa dabbed the corners of her mouth and then took a long swallow of cola. Glancing at Nathan, she saw immediately that the playfulness had faded from his eyes. She stiffened. "I have a feeling I'm about to lose my job."

"You know the job is your dad's to claim whenever he's ready." Keeping his eyes lowered, Nathan reached across the space between them to cradle Filipa's hand. "It's time you started looking toward your own future, don't you think?"

She pictured those four wide-eyed guitar students, and

her heart gave a little thrill. "Believe me, Nathan, I think about it all the time."

"Then I want you to go somewhere with me on Monday. There's someone I want you to meet."

"Monday? I don't finish here until noon, and then my father has his PT appointment."

"We could do this while he's at his appointment." Nathan ran his thumb across her fingertips.

She tried not to flinch when he grazed a sore spot. "What's this all about? Something to do with the cook-off?"

"Not the cook-off. You. Your future. Your . . ." Nathan's voice trailed off. He tugged Filipa's hand closer, turning it to catch the overhead light. Again he traced his thumb across her fingertips, and she sensed the moment he knew. Eyes shining, he lifted his head and grinned. "You're playing again. Fil, you're playing again!"

Flames licked her neck. She yanked her hand away. "It's not a big deal, okay?"

"Are you kidding? It's a *very* big deal." Nathan inched his chair closer, this time seizing both her hands. "That's exactly why you have to come with me on Monday."

"I told you, it's out of the question."

"I'm telling you, Fil, nothing you're doing on Monday can possibly be more important that this meeting."

Her eyes narrowed. "What have you done?"

Nathan drew in a long, slow breath. "I've found another music school for you. One where you can study music the way it was meant to be played—from the heart. From *your* heart. No pedantic perfectionists, just music instructors who encourage creativity and freedom of expression."

Filipa's jaw tensed. She slid her hands free and tucked

them against her sides. "*You* decided this? Without talking to *me* first?"

"I wanted to surprise you." Oblivious to her rising annoyance, Nathan continued on. "It's all set, Fil. Janet Locker is the dean of a small but very prestigious music conservatory in Baltimore, and she's flying in on Monday to meet you and hear you play." His mouth spread into an excited grin. "It's perfect—you've already been practicing. And she's open to discussing financial aid—"

"Stop. Just stop! I told you a thousand times, I am *not* going back to music school." Filipa shoved her chair back. So taken aback that she could hardly speak, she pushed to her feet. Her next words came out on an angry sob. "How dare you treat me like one more problem to solve! This is my *life*, not one of your business deals."

"But I thought—"

"No, you didn't think at all." Doubt and confusion raging, she marched to the door and slammed it behind her.

Chapter Sixteen

Well, he couldn't say Sheridan hadn't warned him. Still numb from Filipa's reaction, Nathan decided he'd better focus on damage control. First order of business? Explain the situation to Janet Locker. "I'm sorry for inconveniencing you. I'll reimburse you for whatever fees are involved in canceling your flight."

"I'm certainly disappointed. Is there no chance Miss Beltran will change her mind?"

"Not by Monday, that's for sure." Nathan apologized again and said goodbye.

Sinking into the sofa cushions, he jammed his fists into his eye sockets. *Stupid, stupid, stupid!* He should have spent more time praying and less time interfering. Would Fil ever forgive him?

When she didn't join him at Kingsley Faith Fellowship Sunday morning, he figured she was avoiding him. When Manuelo called that evening to say he would return to work on Monday, Nathan decided Filipa just needed a few days to cool off. When he left a voicemail offering Filipa a ride to the weekly fundraiser committee meeting, she didn't return his call. So by Thursday, after Filipa hadn't even shown up for the riding classes she'd been helping with, Nathan was convinced she never wanted to see him again.

The following Monday, he met with Kip in the study to review the latest horse management expenditures. They'd been going over invoices and price lists for nearly an hour when Kip suddenly slammed a drawer shut.

Nathan jumped, sending a stack of papers tumbling off his lap. "What'd you do that for?"

"Just seein' if you're awake. You've been staring at the same page for ten minutes."

"Sorry. Where were we?" Nathan bent down to retrieve the papers.

"The real question is, where are *you*?" Kip pushed aside the equine supply catalogues he'd been going through. "You've been walkin' around in a daze for at least a week now. I'm gonna throw out a wild guess here and say this must have something to do with Filipa."

Groaning, Nathan leaned his elbows on the desk and propped his head in his hands. "I've blown it, man. I've totally blown it."

"Figured as much. I've been getting vibes from Sher all week, too. She obviously knows more than she's telling."

If Fil had confided in Sheridan, that was a good thing. At least Nathan hoped so. "Women. I survived a hormonal teenage sister and I still don't understand them. How are you supposed to know when to come to their rescue and when to back off?"

"When in doubt, back off." Chuckling, Kip reached for his coffee cup. "*Then* come to their rescue."

"Ha, ha, you are just a barrelful of good advice." Nathan rose to shove a folder into the file drawer. "I'll look at this stuff later. I've got to get cracking on cook-off business."

Filipa handed Sheridan a chilled can of lemon-lime soda and then sat down next to her on the Beltrans' front steps. "I'm glad you came over. I really miss spending time at the farm."

Sheridan popped the top on her soda can. "Are you ever going to speak to Nathan again?"

"You don't beat around the bush, do you?" Leaning sideways, Filipa cast her friend a crooked smile.

Sheridan sipped her drink, then set the can down on the step. "I know you're in love with him, Fil. Cut him some slack, okay? He only wanted to help."

"He just doesn't get that I've got to figure things out for myself. I've done the music school thing. I'm not sure I could ever go back, even if this place in Baltimore is everything Nathan claimed."

"But do you really want to spend the rest of your life teaching beginners?"

Filipa sighed, her thoughts returning to those bright, smiling faces in Mrs. Hunter's family room. Only three lessons and the kids were insatiable, always pleading to learn one more chord, anxious to try their skills on a new song.

She shifted to face Sheridan. "You've told me before how much you miss teaching—the fulfillment you experienced working with the special-ed kids. And now you're in training for equine therapy instructor certification. So you know what I'm talking about. Nothing in the world compares to the joy of helping a child—any child, learning disabled or otherwise—master a new skill."

With a sad smile, Sheridan grasped Filipa's wrist. "Then tell Nathan. Tell him what you're doing, and why."

"Are you sure he won't just try harder to convince me I'm wasting my 'gift'? I haven't even found the courage to tell my parents yet."

Sheridan's lips slanted in an accusing glare. "You ran away from school because you couldn't take the pressure, then hid out for months doing manual labor at the farm. Now you're playing the guitar again, but you're afraid for anyone to know you're teaching beginners." She huffed. "Filipa Beltran, when are you going to quit running and start living?"

Stunned into silence, Filipa faced forward, lips trembling. She *had* been afraid—afraid of being judged a failure, afraid of letting down the people she loved most. Sheridan was right. It was time to stop running away. It was time to be honest with herself, with her family, and with Nathan.

Sheridan left a few minutes later, leaving Filipa plenty to think about. She sat on the porch step a long while afterward, trying her best to stop telling God all the reasons she couldn't be the "perfect" daughter/sister/student/musician she assumed everyone expected her to be, but instead to open her heart fully to the Spirit's direction. *You gave me the gift of music for a reason, Lord. Show me how You want me to use it. Not my will but Yours be done.*

Feeling more at peace, she pushed up from the step and went inside. She found her father in the living room, an ice pack on his knee. "Papa, are you hurting?"

"Not bad, but perhaps I did more than I should have this morning."

Filipa plopped onto the sofa across from him. "I should

be helping you. I shouldn't have let you start back on your own so soon."

"No. What you *should* be doing—I am sorry, but I can be silent about this no longer—is returning to school to continue your music studies." The corners of Papa's mouth turned down in an exasperated frown. "*Mija*, when will this nonsense end?"

So much for those few moments of peace. She extended her hands to show him the newly forming calluses. "I'm playing again. I have been for a couple of weeks." As his eyebrows rose in a look of grateful surprise, she explained about teaching the small class of Down syndrome children. "I love it, Papa. These kids fulfill me more than any concert performance ever did or ever could."

"I see." Glancing toward the carpet, her father rubbed his chin. "But could you not accomplish so much more as a teacher if you earn your degree? You were so close."

True, when she left school last summer, she lacked only a few credit hours to complete her bachelor's in music performance, and her advisor had already set things in motion toward enrolling her in the master's program. Papa was right—she owed it to herself, and to the people who had put so much faith in her, to at least finish her degree.

Rising, she planted a kiss on her father's temple. "I'll think about it, Papa. I promise."

At least she no longer had to practice in secret. Later, when the whole family sat down for supper together, Filipa told them all what she had been doing for the past few weeks. The younger kids kept right on eating while rattling on about their school day. Charlie paused long enough in his chewing to mutter, "Cool."

But Mama beamed with thoughtful pride. "This is a

good thing. Sharing your gift with others is the best way to honor the Giver."

Buoyed by her parents' understanding and support, and more certain than ever of God's direction, Filipa pondered her next step—making things right with Nathan.

Nathan would be so relieved to have this cook-off behind him. Maybe then he could finally take the time he needed to make things right with Fil.

Standing at the head of the conference table, he passed out agendas. "It's crunch time, people. The cook-off is a week from Saturday, so tonight we need to make sure all the bases are covered."

He glanced toward the spot where Filipa had been sitting the past few weeks and tried not to think about how much he missed her.

Tried not to think about what an arrogant, know-it-all jerk he'd been.

Because no matter how good he was at managing an equine therapy center or spearheading a fundraiser or keeping a committee meeting on track, Filipa was right—he couldn't solve her problems for her, and he'd been a fool to even try.

Drawing his focus to the business at hand, Nathan somehow made it through the meeting. Three hours later, confident they were as ready as they'd ever be, he and Sheridan walked out to the church parking lot.

Stepping out the door, Nathan noticed wet pavement glimmering under the streetlights. He glanced toward the sky, where scudding clouds blotted out the stars. "Did you realize it had rained?"

Sheridan sidestepped a puddle. "Never heard a thing. Must have been a passing shower."

"I hope that's all it was, or else Kip was real busy with Jet."

As they arrived at the farm, Nathan could see it had rained much harder out this way. Seeing Manuelo's pickup parked near the barn door, Nathan grimaced. "Uh-oh. Kip must have called for help."

Sheridan shoved open the passenger door. "I hope neither one of them did anything stupid."

Nathan stopped at the cottage long enough to toss his briefcase and keys inside before catching up with Sheridan in the barn. Walking on through, they followed the sounds of classical music drifting from the small barn beyond. Nathan spotted Kip first. The cowboy lounged on a hay bale, a piece of straw captured between his teeth and his Stetson pulled low over his face.

Easing forward, Nathan caught Sheridan's sleeve. "Is he . . . asleep?"

"I don't—" Sheridan froze and clutched Nathan's arm. "Oh, Nathan, look!"

Stepping farther into the small barn, Nathan peered into the dim interior. A shadowy figure came into view across from Jet's stall, and Nathan's heart stuttered—*Fil!*

Tranquil as a rippling stream, the soft, gentle music flowed from her guitar. She played with her eyes closed, a look of rapture brightening her features. Nathan peered into Jet's stall at the most relaxed animal he'd ever seen. Stretched out on his side in the shavings, Jet looked as comfortable and unconcerned as an old dog in front of a cozy fire.

The music suddenly stopped. "Nathan! I didn't hear you."

He stepped hesitantly toward the woman he loved. "Keep playing. It's beautiful."

Filipa stood, the guitar cradled against her. She cast a timid glance past Nathan's shoulder.

Behind him he heard Kip stirring. "Huh? Must've dozed off. What time is it?"

"Don't mind us, you two," Sheridan said. "Come on, cowboy, let's get you to bed."

Nathan couldn't tear his eyes off Filipa long enough to acknowledge his sister and brother-in-law. He moved closer. "I've missed you so much, Fil. I'm sorry. I was so wrong."

"I'm sorry, too. I overreacted that day. I've done a lot of soul searching since then, and I think I'm finally getting my head on straight."

"Looks pretty straight to me." He caressed her cheek. "Please say you forgive me, Fil. Give me another chance, and I promise I'll never try to run your life again."

She chuckled softly, her hand covering his as she leaned into his touch. Her mouth tipped upward in a questioning smile. "Not even if I want you to?"

At his confused stammer, she guided him over to a tack trunk and pulled him down beside her. Hesitantly she confided in him about the day she'd driven into Charlotte intent on selling her guitar, only to end up teaching lessons to four children with Down syndrome. "Music has never made me happier than when I'm working with those kids," she said, amazement filling her voice. "Three years working toward a music performance degree convinced me I'm not cut out for the concert stage. The nerves, the long days and late nights, the stress of going on tour—it's not for me."

"But you're so good, Fil. Your talent could take you anywhere you want to go."

"It won't be back to New York, I can guarantee you

that. But I do need to finish my degree—or rather, switch gears and start working toward a different major."

"And that would be . . . ?"

"Music therapy. Teaching kids like Debby, maybe even incorporating a music component into therapeutic riding —imagine the possibilities!"

The thrill in her eyes blazed straight through Nathan's heart. "Wow. That would be amazing!"

"I looked online at that school in Baltimore you were so enthusiastic about, and they offer an excellent music therapy program." Casting Nathan a shy glance, she drew her lower lip between her teeth. "I was hoping there might still be a chance to audition."

Nathan's emotional roller-coaster careened around another corner. He'd barely allowed himself to enjoy the idea of having Filipa around permanently, and now she was talking about going away again.

Don't forget this was your idea, wise guy.

He swiveled away, hands clutched between his knees. "Yeah, sure. I'll contact Ms. Locker."

"Nathan, what's wrong?" Her fingers wriggled into the space between his palms. "Isn't this what you wanted?"

A ragged breath tore from his lungs. "What I wanted— what I *want*—is this." He scooped her into his arms and kissed her until he thought his heart would explode. Her lips were warm and pliant, their sweetness making him hungry for more. How could he bear to wait a year or two or three until she came home again? How could he survive without her?

She drew back slowly, eyes shining, quick breaths pulsing the air between them. "I want this, too, Nathan, more than you know." She brushed his lips with the tips of her fingers, and he shivered. "Baltimore isn't nearly as far away as New York. I'd come home often. I promise."

Heat filled Nathan's chest. His fingers tangled in Filipa's mass of thick, ebony tresses, and he buried his face against her neck. Inhaling the sweet scent of jasmine, he murmured, "Good. Because every day we're apart is going to feel like a century."

Chapter Seventeen

"Thank you so much for arranging this, Ms. Locker." Guitar on her lap, Filipa perched on a straight-backed chair in Nathan's cottage and smiled into the webcam on Nathan's laptop.

"Thank Nathan." The woman's image in the videoconferencing window was just slightly out of sync with her spoken words. She gave an easy laugh. "That young man is nothing if not persistent."

Filipa glanced toward Nathan, seated on her right. It was the Monday before the big fundraiser event, and yet he'd sacrificed valuable time to set up this video audition. His staunch belief in her, his unwavering support, his willingness to give her this chance even if it meant they'd be apart for a while—love and gratitude swelled her heart.

"Anytime you're ready, Miss Beltran."

For the audition Filipa had selected *Saltarello*, by Vincenzo Galilei, a lively piece she felt would best showcase her mastery. With a bolstering breath she adjusted her posture and began to play.

The song ended, and Filipa sat motionless as she

awaited Ms. Locker's response. The image on the video screen wavered, making the woman's expression unreadable. Finally she spoke. "Miss Beltran, your skills—no, your *gift*—would unquestionably qualify you for any area of music you should choose to pursue. It would be a distinct pleasure to start the wheels in motion for your transfer to our conservatory."

Wishing she could scream with delight, Filipa managed a dignified but heartfelt "Thank you." Out of range of the webcam she grabbed Nathan's hand and squeezed it. She gladly allowed Nathan to join the conversation, and by the time the videoconference ended, they'd arranged for Filipa to begin her music therapy studies with a couple of short-term distance-learning courses she could begin immediately.

After packing away her guitar, Filipa wrapped her arms around Nathan. "It feels as if my life is finally starting to make sense!"

"I know mine sure is." The smile never left his face even as he tilted his head to kiss her.

With a sigh, she nestled deeper against his chest. "I don't know how I'll manage finances, though. Changing schools will probably mean losing most of my scholarships."

"You heard Ms. Locker. She's almost positive the board will authorize at least partial assistance." Nathan brushed his lips across her forehead. "Stop worrying. If this is God's plan for you, it'll all work out."

Though she felt more certain than ever that she was following God's plan, Filipa knew all too well the financial struggles her parents endured as Mexican immigrants. Worry? She couldn't help but worry. Easing out of

Nathan's arms, she stroked the lid of her guitar case. "Maybe I should try again to sell my guitar."

"No way!" Nathan's vehemence surprised her.

"But why not? Going into music therapy, there's no reason I'd need an instrument of this caliber."

"Because . . ." He stepped between her and the case, his fingers closing around her upper arms with gentle urgency. "Because someone believed so strongly in you and your music that he wanted you to have the very best guitar money could buy. It was a gift, Fil. Just like your music is a gift. And you don't refuse a gift, okay?"

"Okay, I'll keep my Paulino Bernabe." Puzzled by the intensity behind Nathan's words, Filipa reached up to smooth away the frown lines marring his cheek. If she didn't know better, she'd think maybe Nathan was her anonymous benefactor.

Then, with a sudden stab of certainty, she knew— *Nathan's father.* As generous as the Crosses had been to the Beltrans in a thousand other ways, how could it have been anyone else? Thanks to him, and thanks to Nathan, a fresh start now lay before her, bright like sunlight glimmering on an open highway. And in the rearview mirror of her mind, she glimpsed unmistakable evidence of God's hand in every moment that had brought her to this point—not the least of which was falling wildly in love with Nathan Cross.

"Come here, big guy." She slid her hand behind his neck and drew him toward her for another kiss—only to be interrupted by the jarring marimba sounds of his cell phone.

Their lips parted, and Nathan breathed out a reluctant sigh. "Hold that thought." Snatching his phone off the end table, he scanned the Caller ID. His eyes spoke apology as he said, "It's Karen Cardenas. Must be cook-off business."

Filipa plopped down on the ottoman and hoped the call wouldn't take too long. As she listened to Nathan's side of the conversation, his tone grew serious. She quickly gathered the news wasn't good. Disconnecting, he collapsed into the overstuffed chair behind her with a groan.

She swung around, resting her palm on his knee. "What did Karen say?"

Nathan scraped a hand down his face. "Our bluegrass band just cancelled."

"Oh, no! What happened?"

"They were on their way to a gig Saturday night and got rear-ended. Two of the guys are in the hospital." At Filipa's gasp, he went on, "They're gonna be fine, just laid up for a while. But there goes our entertainment for the cook-off."

Nathan didn't have to explain that with the event only a few days away, it would be next to impossible to book another group. He looked so stricken that Filipa's heart ached for him. "Nathan, I'm sorry. I wish—"

She bit the inside of her cheek as a wild idea flashed through her mind. Not exactly a replacement bluegrass band, but it could work. Rising, she moved to the arm of his chair and rested her head against his. "Let me take care of the entertainment, okay? I promise you won't be disappointed."

Offering only a reassuring smile at his confused stare, she gathered up her purse and guitar case and fled the cottage.

Half an hour and several phone calls later, she'd set her plan in motion.

No matter how many times he asked, Nathan couldn't get Filipa to tell him anything. He wondered if maybe *she* was the entertainment she was lining up, but she'd made it crystal clear that she'd never cared much for performing onstage. Besides, he couldn't quite get his head around a classical guitarist playing at a barbecue cook-off.

But with only a few days left to prepare for the big day, Nathan's brain was on overload with a million other concerns. At least now he had his mother and Tom to help. They'd driven up Wednesday afternoon in Tom's massive RV. His barbecue team followed in a dually pickup towing a big, black smoker on wheels.

Mom slid easily into her former role as the matriarch of Cross Roads Farm, and neither Nathan nor Sheridan objected in the least. Extra volunteers joined them on Friday to start setting up for the cook-off, and by noon Saturday the farm had been transformed. The two front pastures had been opened up and marked off for parking. Savory aromas rose in a smoky haze from the barbecue trailers lining the perimeter of the arena, and three dozen round tables with red-checked tablecloths filled the space inside. The farm hadn't looked this festive since Mom and Sheridan's double wedding last August.

Shortly after four, Nathan, Sheridan, and their mother stood at the arena entrance to welcome their first guests, the five local dignitaries who had agreed to judge the cook-off.

"Did I mention my husband's team is among the contenders?" Nathan's mother asked sweetly as she shook the mayor's hand. "Not that I'd want to influence you or anything."

Mayor Richards chuckled. "What are we gonna do with you, Linda—lettin' yourself be corrupted by that beef-eatin' Texan!"

She winked. "We'll see if you're still talking like that after you sample Tom's mesquite-smoked brisket topped with his special brown-sugar barbecue sauce."

As the tables started filling up with ticket holders, Nathan glanced toward the empty stage. Filipa had requested five chairs and five microphones, but he still had no idea what she'd planned. And since she hadn't shown up yet, he was starting to get nervous.

Spotting Rosa Beltran and her daughter Naomi helping set up the buffet table, he sidled over. "Any idea when Filipa will get here?"

Rosa answered with a tight-lipped smile as she placed a serving spoon beside a large aluminum container of potato salad. "I'm sure she is on her way."

"Nathan." Sheridan came up from behind and grabbed his elbow. "You need to get onstage and do your welcome speech. It's time to get started."

Flicking another anxious glance toward the arena entrance, Nathan flattened his lips and marched to the stage. He removed the center microphone from its stand. "Hey, folks—or, for our Texas visitors, howdy! I'm Nathan Cross. On behalf of all the staff and volunteers at Cross Roads Farm, thanks for coming. Our equine therapy program was my dad's dream, and I know he'd be mighty proud to see you all here to support us."

Nathan spoke briefly about the history and purpose of the program, then introduced his mother, Sheridan and Kip, Manuelo and family, and other key staff members and volunteers. "We'd also like to thank His Honor Ben Richards, mayor of Kingsley, for heading up our judges' panel."

When the applause died away, Nathan brought Pastor Alan Wolfe onstage to offer a prayer, then invited the guests to proceed to the buffet. As he turned to step off the stage, he saw Filipa weaving her way through the tables. He whooshed out a huge sigh of relief. "There you are! I was getting worried."

She grinned. "Aren't you the one always telling *me* not to worry? Now introduce me so the entertainment can begin."

Nathan snapped his gaping jaw closed and started to the microphone, only to halt mid-stride and swing back toward Filipa. "Uh, what should I say? And you did ask for five chairs. Where's everybody else?"

"Never mind. Just introduce us as 'Filipa and friends.'" She waved him on.

Taking the microphone again, Nathan tried not to stammer. "Ladies and gentlemen, sorry to interrupt, but, uh . . . please welcome Filipa . . ." He glanced over his shoulder, and she gave a reassuring nod as she took the center chair. "Filipa and . . . friends." He just hoped the "friends" would show up soon because right now he was feeling like a bumbling idiot.

He hadn't gone five steps before a guitar version of "Sweet Caroline" poured from the speakers. Spinning around, he gaped at the woman from whose fingers such spirited music flowed. Several bars later she segued into "Sweet Home Alabama," and from there into "Georgia on My Mind," and finally "The Yellow Rose of Texas." By the time the montage ended, the guests were clapping and humming along.

Carrying a plate of barbecue, Sheridan drew up beside Nathan. "That's *our* Fil? I thought she only played classical."

Nathan shook his head in amazement. "Me, too."

He watched as Filipa shifted in her chair and adjusted

the microphone. Her next chords were hauntingly tender, an old tune that took Nathan back to his childhood and listening in secret from a horse stall as Filipa practiced her guitar in the hayloft. Her voice rose in a delicate tremolo as she sang along to "Blowin' in the Wind."

Lost in the sound and the memories, Nathan almost didn't notice when a second voice and guitar joined Filipa's. A young girl with curly blond hair and almond-shaped eyes sidled onto the stage and took the chair on Filipa's right. By the second verse another child came onstage, and then another and another, all looking to be about twelve years old.

Filipa's Down syndrome guitar students—of course! The song ended, and the crowd erupted with cheers and applause. Nathan's heart was so full that he could hardly catch his breath. "Filipa and friends" had just stolen the show.

"You were all simply wonderful!" Surrounded by her students at the foot of the stage, Filipa gave each of them a huge hug. When she'd first approached them with the idea of performing at the cook-off, she hadn't known what to expect.

But their enthusiasm—and their parents'—had nearly bowled her over. The girls had worked extra hard that Monday on the songs she'd been teaching them, and then met to practice again on Wednesday and Friday. While their playing lacked precision, these kids gave new meaning to making a joyful noise to the Lord.

She gasped when two strong arms wrapped around her from behind. Nathan's warm breath whispered against her ear. "This was absolutely the best entertainment we could have asked for. You're amazing, Fil."

Whirling around within the circle of his embrace, she smiled up at him. "It's the kids who are amazing. Do you see now why they make me so happy?"

"Oh, yeah." He rocked her gently side-to-side. "And do you see now why you make *me* so happy?"

Her pulse skittered. She stared at his shirt button. "Um, maybe you should remind me."

He tilted her chin up, his lips moving closer, and then—

"Miss Fil, Miss Fil!" Debby's shrill voice snapped them both out of the moment. "Is he your boyfriend?"

The other girls giggled, hands covering their mouths. "Is he? Is he?"

While Filipa tried not to blush, Nathan held her close to his side in a possessive gesture. "You betcha I'm her boyfriend." He gazed down at Filipa, his tone mellowing. "Actually, I was wondering if we could change that to *fiancé*. You good with that? Just temporarily, of course. Because I've got something a lot more permanent in mind not too far down the road."

The words, combined with his teasing smile, zinged through her like an electrical shock. Fully aware of the girls' curious stares, she swallowed over the sudden tightness in her throat. Then, gathering her senses, she arched her neck and shot Nathan a cool stare. "If that's your idea of a proposal, I believe you're in need of some serious romantic intervention."

"Oh, it's romance you want. Well, then . . ." Nathan swept her into a dip and proceeded to kiss the living daylights out of her, until she thought she'd fade into a genuine old-fashioned swoon.

Laughter, applause, and catcalls rang in her ears. She knew she must have said yes at some point, but after that kiss, everything else was only a blur. She vaguely remembered Nathan announcing the fundraiser had brought in close to $16,000. Someone reminded her later that a barbecue team from Fort Mill, South Carolina, had taken first place, barely beating out Tom Jacobs's Texas-style beef brisket.

But what she'd remember for the rest of her life was seeing the love in Nathan's eyes and realizing God's gifts didn't get any better than this.

Are you ready for the next book in the series?
Look for Grace and Ryan's story in book 3,
A Horseman's Hope

If you enjoyed *A Horseman's Gift*, please spread the word among your reader friends and wherever you share about books on Facebook, Goodreads, Instagram, or other social media.

Reviews are always deeply appreciated. A review doesn't have to be lengthy or eloquent, just a few brief words sharing your honest impressions. Reviews and personal recommendations are the best ways to help authors get discovered by new readers.

To receive regular updates about Myra Johnson's books and special events, subscribe to her newsletter (signup form on website, http://myrajohnson.com/newsletter-signup/).

Visit Myra online:
www.myrajohnson.com

After a five-year sojourn in Oklahoma, then eight years in the beautiful Carolinas, native Texan Myra Johnson and her husband are happy to be home once again in the Lone Star State enjoying wildflowers, Tex-Mex, and real Texas barbecue! Myra has been writing stories for as long as she can remember. Her published novels have garnered many awards, including top honors in Christian Retailing's Best for historical fiction and the National Excellence in Romance Fiction Awards. Her books have also earned acclaim in the ACFW Carol Awards, Georgia Romance Writers Maggie Awards, Selah Awards, and Faith, Hope and Love Christian Writers Reader's Choice Awards.

Married for 50-plus years, Myra and her husband have two beautiful daughters married to wonderful Christian men, plus seven amazing grandchildren and a beautiful great-granddaughter. The Johnsons share their home with two pampered rescue dogs and a snobby but lovable cat they inherited from their younger daughter when the family moved overseas.

To receive regular updates about Myra's books and other news, be sure to subscribe to her newsletter (signup form on website).

Find Myra online:
www.myrajohnson.com

facebook.com/MyraJohnsonAuthor

x.com/MyraJohnson

instagram.com/mjwrites

bookbub.com/authors/myra-johnson

goodreads.com/MyraJohnsonAuthor

pinterest.com/mjwrites

FLOWERS OF EDEN HISTORICAL SERIES

The Sweetest Rain

Castles in the Clouds

A Rose So Fair

TILL WE MEET AGAIN HISTORICAL SERIES

When the Clouds Roll By

Whisper Goodbye

Every Tear a Memory

CONTEMPORARY WOMEN'S FICTION

All She Sought[1]

One Imperfect Christmas

The Soft Whisper of Roses

NOVELLAS

The Oregon Trail Romance Collection: Settled Hearts

Designs on Love

Lifetime Investment

---

1. Previously published as *Pearl of Great Price*; see author website for details